blood brother

Michael Simmons

SCHOLASTIC

Scholastic Children's Books,
Euston House, 24 Eversholt Street,
London NW1 1DB, UK
a division of Scholastic Ltd
London ~ New York ~ Toronto ~ Sydney ~ Auckland
Mexico City ~ New Delhi ~ Hong Kong

First published in the US by Roaring Brook Press, 2006

First published in the UK by Scholastic Ltd, 2006

Copyright © Michael Simmons, 2006
Cover images © Getty Images

10 digit ISBN 0 439 96379 6
13 digit ISBN 978 0439 96379 4

Printed in Denmark by Nørhaven Paperback A/S

10 9 8 7 6 5 4 3 2 1

The right of Michael Simmons to be identified as the author of
this work has been asserted by him in accordance with the
Copyright, Designs and Patents Act, 1988.

Papers used by Scholastic Children's Books are made from wood grown in
sustainable forests.

The author wishes to thank

Thaddeus Bower,
Anne Dahlie,
Elizabeth Dahlie,
Susan Dahlie,
Allison Lynn,
George Nicholson,
Neal Porter, and
Paul Rodeen.

EVERY MAN has a talent. This, at least, is what my father always told me. Of course I usually dismissed this sort of statement as the kind of fatherly advice I could do without. But the fact is that I do have a talent, one really good talent, which is that I'm an excellent guitar player. I imagine that one day this talent will bring me great fame and fortune. Seems very likely, in fact. But so far, the most it ever landed me was the role of lead guitarist in a band that impersonated the rock band KISS. The band was called KISS FOREVER. I dressed up like Ace Frehley—KISS's lead guitarist—and entertained clubfuls of screaming KISS fans willing to fork over twenty bucks and believe in our illusion for a night. It may sound like kind of a dopey gig. In fact, I can hardly say it was otherwise. All the same, I made money, I played in real clubs, and I was one of the few sixteen-year-olds in the Chicago area that could call himself a working musician. Not bad.

Anyway, all this is important, but mostly irrelevant for right now. This is really a story about my brother. It's a story about my brother and me.

2 BUT I NEED to make another introductory remark.

In case today's man and today's woman has forgotten the rock band KISS, here's a brief description: In the mid-seventies, in the midst of a whirlwind of disco, bell-bottoms, and feathered hair, there arose a musical and theatrical phenomenon known as KISS. I was not alive then, and as far as I can tell, I'm very lucky not to have been. The world was without interesting movies, there was no such thing as e-mail, and no one had even thought of the idea of a CD player. To make matters worse, the people back then were all freaks. Not just some, but all. As I say, I wasn't around. But I really didn't need to be to come to the conclusion that people back then were strange.

The kings of the freaks were KISS, a rock band that was famous for elaborate makeup; tight-fitting black costumes with silver belts; wigs (or what looked like wigs but might well have been real hair given how people looked back then); and onstage antics that included spitting blood, lighting things on fire, and numerous other activities I'm too polite to mention. The lead singer and bass player, a guy named Gene Simmons, was especially famous for an extremely long tongue (extremely long), which he used to hang over his bottom lip and wag at the audience, often as blood dripped from his mouth.

He still does this, as far as I know, although the guy's about a million years old now.

Anyway, there are those who see the band KISS as a definitive phenomenon in the history of American culture. The other guys in my band, who were all in their early thirties and loved KISS more than anything else in the world, said this. The lunatic fans who came to our shows said this. And the crazy people who follow KISS around (when they get back together for concerts) still say this. But not me. I am young enough to have escaped the massive brainwashing that must have occurred before my birth. I am very lucky for this.

So, given my opinions, why did I take the job as the lead guitarist for a KISS tribute band? Well, again, put on a lot of makeup and bang out some heavy-metal and people will pay you money. And as jobs go, playing guitar beat working at the video store or mowing lawns. I got the job when the other band members saw me playing guitar at a local battle-of-the-bands-type event. It's actually kind of a good story. But I'll tell it later. As I say, I'm just offering this background information for the purposes of clarity and historical accuracy. You'll need to know it to follow all this.

Anyway, let me tell you about Jason.

3

I WAS ELEVEN years old and just a budding guitar genius when my brother was first arrested. Actually, he wasn't officially arrested. He was just corralled by the cops and brought to our house in a squad car. His offense was pretty idiotic. A neighbor had just had a new lawn put in—the kind that comes on the back of a truck in sheets and is laid down piece by piece. Late at night, on a whim, my bother and a few of his friends decided to pull up the sheets of turf. They had torn the lawn to shreds by the time the cops showed up. The boys ran, but the cops caught them. The neighbor was a family friend of ours. She said that she didn't want to press charges. She knew some of the boys' parents—my parents especially—and said that she would handle their punishment. She just asked that the cops bring the boys home.

When my parents met the police at the door, they could barely speak. My mother was trying not to cry and my dad was trying not to scream. When the cops left, Jason was ordered into the living room. They were in there for about two hours, yelling the whole time.

In the next few years, this kind of event would become routine. In fact, I think my parents wished that Jason would go back to tearing up lawns for fun. He started doing things that were much, much worse. But the worse he got, the more my parents learned to take his behavior in stride. They got to know the police pretty well, and my mother stopped crying when they showed up at the door. Finally, late one spring, Jason got busted for spray-painting his name on the back of a grocery store and then starting a fire in the store's garbage Dumpster, which quickly spread to the store's roof. He was seventeen. When the judge asked him why he did it, he said he didn't know. That's what he always said. He said he didn't know why he did what he did and that he was sorry. The judge decided that it was time Jason paid some real penalties for his actions. He sent Jason to a juvenile detention center for the summer.

"I don't have any patience for this kind of vandalism," the judge said. "Still, I'm hoping you can clean up your act by the beginning of the next school year."

"I want to do that," Jason replied. "And I'm sorry for what I did."

Such apologies were kind of unexplainable given the fact that he never changed. But Jason really was sorry. That was always the sad thing. The sad true thing. He really was always sorry.

4 **SO THE SUMMER** that Jason was in "juvie" was a summer of peace. It was a peaceful summer. When Jason wasn't setting fire to local businesses, he was spending his time tormenting me. Here are three examples of this. (There are more. These aren't even the worst things he did to me. But they'll give you a basic sense of what it was like living with him.)

1) I once spent eleven days building a model of the Alamo out of balsa wood, papier-mâché, and Styrofoam for an end-of-the-year school project. The day after I completed the project, the day it was due, I awoke to discover the model in pieces. My brother confessed. Said he was sorry even. He said he had knocked it off the dining room table in the middle of the night while he was getting a drink of water. He said he fell on it and that he was sorry it happened, but that if you really thought about it, it wasn't his fault. It was dark. He was sleepy.

If there was even a shred of a possibility that it was an accident, I would have forgiven him. But the model was completely and entirely destroyed. No way just falling on it could bust it into so many pieces. It must have taken him half an hour to do such a thoroughly destructive job.

2) There was this woman I liked—Amanda—and much of my life was spent scheming about how to go out with her. Much of Jason's life was spent trying to sabotage this plan, just as he tried to sabotage everything in my life. Anyway, there was this one time that I finally got up the guts to call Amanda and ask her out. It was hard work. I'm kind of a coward. But there was this end-of-the-year dance and everyone else seemed to be bringing a date, so I figured this might be the time to bite the bullet. Anyway, I alerted my family to my upcoming important actions, insisted that everyone leave me alone while I was on the phone, and then called her up. So, not three minutes into our conversation, which, admittedly, was filled with me stammering and saying fairly stupid things, Jason picked up the other phone and said, "Have you told Amanda you love her yet, lover-boy?"

What was there for me to say? I know when I've been humiliated, and I certainly had no idea how to recover from such a horrifying incident. I quickly hung up the phone. No goodbyes. I just hung up. Just like that. True, I did not handle the situation very well, but my life was a long string of such inexplicable decisions. Unfortunate. Still, also not entirely my fault. With a guy like Jason in your life, there are all sorts of ways to mess up.

3) I had a friend (nicknamed "Fitz") over after school one day. I was younger. About ten. We decided to play Monopoly, and Jason insisted on joining in. He was eleven then— not yet in trouble with the police, but certainly already tormenting me. Anyway, we played Monopoly and Fitz won. Fair and square. Beat me and Jason. But Jason got so mad that he not only knocked over the board, but he then proceeded to beat Fitz to a pulp. Knocked out a tooth even. When my mother asked what all the fighting was about, Jason stared at my friend and then started screaming that he hated my friend and that he hated me and that he hated Monopoly and that he hated everything in the world. Very strange. So strange that my friend stopped crying. Blood was coming out of his mouth and he just stood staring at Jason in this state of bewilderment, like he was thinking, "What the hell is he screaming about? I'm the one with the missing tooth." Again, very strange.

But let me say one more thing. I got treated pretty badly by Jason. He never set me on fire, but he was pretty mean to me. All the same, there was part of me that desperately wanted him to like me. And there were times that he did, that he did seem to like me. And as strange as it seems, that kind of affection, as rare as it was, was totally gripping, totally captivating to me. Troubling though, because it came and went so quickly. Anyway, kind of important for you to know.

5   **I ALSO HAD** a sister named Olivia. She was really the only one in my family that I liked. OK. Not true. I liked my mother and father, and I've already described my strange fascination with Jason. But my feelings toward the other family members were riddled with the typical frustration you feel with any family member. Your mom and dad can be the best parents in the world and still drive you crazy. I had good parents. No question about that. All the same, I couldn't spend too much time with them without losing my mind.

The way that I was close with Olivia was different in the sense that there were no downsides to her. She was four years younger than me, and she offered nothing but fun and attention. I could play video games for eight hours straight with her and she'd never get bored. Of course, I was much better and I always beat her. But she was a pretty good sport about it. Perhaps an older brother should let his younger sister win occasionally. But I was interested in training her, in helping her to become a truly excellent video-game player. So letting her win would have defeated my purposes. Had to make her strong.

"You always win," she'd say.

"Life is hard," I'd reply, "and some punk on the street isn't going to cut you any breaks when he challenges you to Madden NFL Football."

Sounds harsh, but I had to be tough. I had to show her tough love.

Aside from palling around with me, Olivia liked to dance. She took a million dance classes and was always being shuttled from one class to another by my parents. We were also always racing around to attend her recitals. This was the one sort of family outing Jason attended without putting up a fight. He liked Olivia a lot too.

My mom also spent a lot of time making Olivia's outfits. You'd never believe how many costumes a kid who dances needs. That's the advantage of being in KISS FOREVER. I needed only one outfit and I was done, although the outfit was pretty complicated. My mother also made it for me, which I never admitted to anyone because it's not very rock 'n' roll to have your mother sewing for you. The other guys in the band all made their own. In my opinion, that's much weirder than having your mom do it. But the guys were pretty proud of their work. Talked about their sewing progress all the time. Mended rips and replaced missing sequins the minute they noticed them. This is something I don't think the original members of KISS spent much time doing, although you never know. As I've said, they were freaks.

Whatever. Olivia was an unblemished, totally enchanting, completely exciting member of our family. A real burst of sunshine, as they say. I couldn't think of a thing bad to say about her, even if I wanted to.

6 SO HERE'S what Jason looked like, just in case you've begun to wonder. He was tall and broad, and pretty athletic. And because he was so big, he was pretty threatening. There were bigger guys in school, and some who were more athletic than him, but in a fight they wouldn't (and didn't) stand much of a chance. Jason had little regard for his own well-being, so people who knew him would quickly back down from a confrontation, seeing that it's pretty scary to fight a guy who's not afraid of getting hurt. Not that I've been in

that many fights in my life. I am a man of peace. But I definitely know the difference between a guy like Jason and some muscle-bound athlete who just thinks he's a tough guy.

Overall, I'd say that Jason's appearance never did him any favors in the larger scheme of things. It might have given him an edge with the other hooligans around town, but it didn't win him any friends amongst the various cops and teachers he interacted with. I'd say that most people would say he was good-looking, but he was also generally a mess. His dark brown hair was always kind of shaggy, and he liked clothes that made him look like he had spent the weekend sleeping in a ditch. And he had this mischievous, conniving grin—he could smile broadly at you but make you feel like you were about to get clubbed in the head.

Anyway, I guess that's enough of a description. But since we're on the topic, I might as well tell you about the way I looked. I'd say, with some regret, that while I might be mildly appealing, I'm not entirely handsome. I have a few of what might be considered physical flaws, although perhaps they're merely flaws to those who do not appreciate the unique, the subtle, and the mysterious.

Were an unsophisticated person to list my flaws, they would probably include large ears, my lack of impressive muscle tone, my occasional clumsiness (I am occasionally clumsy), and maybe some other things that I don't really want to admit to. But let me recast the description as I'm sure certain sympathetic and poetic women in Kensington High often do: "Will Brenner is a towering piece of man who's all that and more." I seem to recall hearing that said about me once, although I may be mistaken about this. In fact, yes, I'm definitely mistaken. I guess that in the end, I'm ordinary looking. Perhaps not a stud, but not really not-a-stud either.

Other general remarks: I was cursed with slow-growing teeth and had braces put on when I was fifteen. Fifteen is only a little over the average braces age, but I would have liked to have taken care of them earlier. It was especially difficult being in a rock band. Not many rock stars these days have braces. Ace Frehley definitely didn't have braces when he was a star. When I first joined KISS FOREVER, that was one thing that troubled the other band members. They liked my guitar playing, but the braces had to go. Unfortunately, they were hard to cover up. Fake teeth didn't cut it. Good ones were really expensive, and anyway, I had to handle backup vocals. Can't be singing backup with false teeth. We finally arrived at a solution: white tape. It wasn't perfect, but from below the stage, no one noticed. And it really wasn't that uncomfortable— I didn't even notice it after a while.

Anyway, the important thing to remember is that I was skinnier and smaller than Jason. And to make matters worse, when Jason returned from juvie that September, he had grown about two more feet. Not good news for an oppressed younger brother.

When he returned, I had actually just been to the mall with my mother and had outfitted myself with some badass new threads for the soon-to-start school year. I was sure to be a hit with the babes. In fact, I was feeling generally cool all around. I was feeling older, wiser, more mature, better dressed, and ready to take on high school with a new sort of bravado. And then my father showed up with Jason after picking him up from his detention camp. Any kind of coolness I was feeling quickly left. Jason was taller, stronger, and his hair was cut really short, like he had been training with the Marines. He hugged my mother and then Olivia. Said he was happy to be back and that he missed all of us. Then he kind of shoved me and laughed.

"You've probably gotten soft without me around, eh, Will?" he said.

The answer to his question was definitely yes. Soft and happy.

But then Jason smiled. And it was kind of a warm smile. For a moment, I even felt like he had a kind of affection for me, might, dare I say, love me like a brother. Still, I knew that one of the many disruptive forces in my life had returned. He quickly shoved me again, this time a little harder. Not hard enough to be identified as an aggressive act, but hard enough to let me know that he was back and that I had better get used to it.

Anyway. Enough background. That September, the September that Jason returned from juvie, is about when the story I'm telling begins. This is really kind of the story of that year. And just in case you've been thinking that I'm a funny, lighthearted guy and that this is going to be a funny story, let me say one more thing: this is a sad story. Really. It's a sad story.

7

MY FATHER happens to be an orthodontist, which is ironic given my malformed teeth. And it's ironic in other ways. Orthodontists make a lot of money. Not millions and millions, but maybe a few million. Maybe an orthodontist can scrape together a few million by the time he dies. I guess the reason that it's slightly ironic is because it's just another example of how stable and smooth our family life was. When someone's having a hard time, you look for reasons. "Why is Jason having such a hard time?" it was often asked. But it was hard to find answers. We had money; my parents loved each other (as far as I could tell); and they spent lots of time, energy, and cash making sure their kids had "all the advantages."

And they were devoted to us. That's no joke. My parents preferred to stay at home helping us with our homework to going to parties or restaurants. I can't really understand this. I'd rather go eat expensive food than do algebra, but such are the mysteries of adulthood.

Anyway, the point is that there were no apparent reasons why Jason should have been such a cutup. And after long periods of thought and careful reflection, there seem to be no hidden reasons either. No one was secretly locking him in a closet at night, no one at school was stupid enough to try to pick on him, and the truth is that the guy wasn't stupid. He didn't do well in school, but his academic failures were more the result of his work habits than his brain power. And don't think anyone ever stopped looking for reasons. I've spent more time in family therapy with Jason than I can calculate, and there were never any answers. Or the answers were always so obvious that you didn't really need a therapist to tell them to you. Like, after hours and hours of jabbering, the therapist would break the astounding news to my parents that "Jason has a hard time behaving."

And I'll say one other thing on this matter: if you're thinking this is a book about how we finally uncovered the mysterious origins of his behavior, let me nix that assumption right now. This is no book about secret psychological motives or the sad true story of how someone ends up being a bully. Jason's behavior was a mystery then and it's still a mystery today.

Whatever. My dad worked about fifteen minutes from the house. He had a pretty big office in the downtown area of Kensington—the suburb of Chicago where we lived—and he shared the office with two other orthodontists. Dad drove a sporty little Toyota, which somehow mirrored everything about my dad. He had the cash to drive an expensive car, but he had a Midwestern fear of flashy objects and could never bring himself to buy anything that was too stylish. It's too bad really. I think there were times that he wanted to own a Porsche and three-thousand-dollar suits. But he could never pull it off and he knew it. Suburban Chicago is no place for Porsche-driving, three-thousand-dollar-suit-wearing high rollers.

Anyway, because my dad's work was somewhat flexible, he arranged with his orthodontist partners to schedule free time to do two things after Jason returned from juvie. First, he took Jason and me to school every morning. Actually, sometimes I walked or hitched a ride with someone else. But my brother always went with my father. It was the one way to be sure that Jason was going to school. The other thing my father did was go to see Jason's probation officer with him. Once a week. Thursday at 3:30. My dad is actually a pretty nice guy, but he can be tough when he wants to be, and he can definitely get mad. He's also very disciplined—a good quality for going through orthodontist school—and he had no problem keeping up his routine with

Jason, even though hauling him around wasn't one of his favorite activities.

There was only one morning that September that the schedule got broken. Jason was sick as a dog with some kind of stomach flu. Even then my dad was banging on his door, telling him to get out of bed.

"No excuses, Jason," he said. "I want you ready in five minutes. You can be sick this afternoon when you get home from school."

Jason basically had to throw up in front of him to prove that he wasn't lying. That was something to see—Jason puking in the upstairs hall while my dad scrambled for towels. I hate to even think about it, and I think my dad felt kind of bad after that.

"All right, bud," he said as he helped him back to bed. "I guess you can't make it today."

The next morning, Jason was out of bed and back in the car with Dad. Convicted arsonists don't get an extra day to lie around and recuperate. If you can walk, you're off to school.

I have to admit that Jason took the whole thing pretty well. You'd think that a guy like Jason might rebel against having his dad drive him to school every day for his senior year. You'd even think that Jason would get pissed about having to meet with his parole officer. But strangely, one of the things that Jason was really good at was taking his punishments without complaint. For instance, before he went to juvie, he used to spend at least two out of five days a week in detention, usually for minor stuff like cutting class or smoking cigarettes. Anyway, he could miss a whole week of class, but somehow always make it to detention. The whole thing was always a mystery to me for a couple of reasons: (a) How could a guy who couldn't find his way to gym class remember with such perfection when he had detention? You'd think detention would be the thing he'd be forgetting. (b) One would imagine he'd clean up his behavior just to avoid having to sit after school for an hour. There were plenty of classes I would have cut without regret except for the detention problem.

Jason deliberately made his life harder. He was like a lab rat that no longer notices when the scientist is shocking him. He got sent to detention over and over without learning a thing about the maze he was navigating every day.

And again, as far as I know, there are no secret explanations for this problem either—there was no girl in detention he was in love with, no detention monitor he wanted to hang around. Jason was just very good at following through with punishments. He was very bad at doing the things that would keep him from being punished in the first place. This quality served him well that September that he returned from juvie. At least as far as making it to school goes. Staying out of detention was another matter. But that September he went only three times, which was something of a record for him.

8 AND, LIKE I MENTIONED, there was also plenty of therapy—individual therapy and family therapy, which had already been happening for some time. It was always a bit annoying, but something we all seemed to get used to. And my parents were very clear that this kind of thing was completely normal, and just exactly what everyone in America ought to do.

"No reason not to talk things out with someone," my father used to say. "Everyone ought to do this."

But it was pretty obvious that we had very specific things to hash out, and that the reason we went was my brother. Start vandalizing grocery stores, and people start to invest in your mental health.

"We've got a lot of work to do," the therapist said when we all reconvened that September. "It's going to be a big year for us."

We all nodded, but no one really looked that hopeful. Frankly, this guy was a little strange. We had first gone to see him a few years earlier when Jason slashed the principal's tires, and the school psychologist strongly recommended family therapy. He had the name of a "great guy," and a week later we were all dressed up in nice clothes, getting introduced.

The guy—Dr. Jones, or "Rick" as he wanted to be called—was nice enough, but he was all dressed in groovy clothes like he was desperately trying to relate to young people. He was in his fifties, but his ear was pierced, he was wearing baggy jeans, and he even had a tattoo—of some kind of flaming crimson heart. He also had long curly hair like he was some kind of 1980s hipster. The problem was this whole look had a vibe to it like he had researched it in some kind of university paper twenty years earlier and that he had determined (after laborious observation) that this was exactly the way to dress if you wanted to "really speak to teens." I mean, I hate to ride him so much for this because, again, he wasn't a bad guy. All the same, he looked completely foolish.

Anyway, that first day back was a funny (and instructive) first meeting, so I'll tell you about it. We all sat in a circle, and the guy asked us to talk about why we thought we were there. My parents gave long-winded parental-type answers that continued with their "everybody needs to talk to someone" routine. My sister said she had no idea why we were there, but she was just as happy here as anywhere else. I said more or less the same thing, although I (shamefully) drifted into my parents' claims that everybody needs therapy. Anyway, we went on like this for a while, until it was clear that the only person who wasn't interested in talking was the supposed reason we were there.

Finally the shrink said, "I haven't heard from Jason yet."

Jason just looked at him and said, "What the hell am I supposed to say?"

"Hey man, you just have to say what you're feeling. Like, whatever your heart and your mind are telling you."

Was this guy joking? This seemed ridiculous, especially because I was now thinking about what my heart and mind were telling me, and they were saying that this guy would go great in my band. He had the KISS FOREVER hair. And he had that overgrown teenager look my middle-aged band mates had. But as usual, given the obvious funny material this guy was providing, Jason beat me to the punch. "Dude," he said. "I actually think I've seen you onstage recently. Are you in KISS FOREVER?"

I immediately started laughing, which made Olivia laugh (and my parents frown), and then the shrink started laughing too, trying to be part of it all.

"Cool, cool," he said, still laughing, and still trying to be down with us. "What's KISS FOREVER?"

"It's just a joke," Jason said.

"I love jokes," the shrink said. "What's the joke?"

My brother looked thoughtful for a moment, like he didn't quite know which direction he was going to take this. Like, there was this look like he just might keep laughing and say that he was having a great time, and that he had no idea that therapy could be so much fun. But there was another side to this look, a side that was kind of pissed off that the shrink was laughing too, a side that wanted to push the dagger in just a little deeper. And that's the direction he took.

"It's actually my brother's band," he said. "They dress up like KISS. They look like freaks. And you're about the freakiest-looking guy I've ever known. So I thought you might have been one of the band members."

The shrink fumbled a bit, then looked deadly serious. "OK, OK," he said, "I'm feeling anger here. Do you want to talk about it? Are you mad that you're back here?"

Very professional. And I'm sure this guy had seen it all before. Try to counsel surly teenagers, and you can hardly expect better. But I'll also tell you this—he was a little surprised. He might have been well trained (and he seemed like a perfectly nice guy, to be honest), but I don't think he took this as lightly as he was trying to pretend. He was rattled.

Anyway, my brother finally replied, "Honestly?" he said. "I'm thinking I want to kick your narrow little ass."

At this point, the shrink frowned a little, and then started quickly jotting notes down in his note-book, like Jason's character had just been fully and deeply revealed to him.

Whatever. We had gone through this kind of thing for years. Kind of shocking really. Not exactly a good use of our time, given that it hardly ever helped. But I think that it did give my parents the sense that they were doing something. I think what was hardest on them, what was most difficult, was that they could never do anything to get Jason to straighten out. Very hard on what you'd call good and caring parents. Led to a lot of guilt, and a lot of very deep frustration. So taking the kid to see a psychologist at least made them feel like something was happening.

But I will say one other thing: for as strange as the shrink could be, and for as hard a time as Jason would give him, Jason liked the guy. I could tell. He liked him better than he liked most adults. For example, as we were all leaving, Jason kind of looked over to him and said (with a kind of touching sincerity and honest regret), "I'm sorry about the 'kicking your ass' comment, man. Just wanted to keep you on your toes."

The shrink suddenly smiled and looked kind of relieved. "Don't worry about that," he said. "I'm happy you're back."

Then Jason smiled, and patted the guy on the shoulder. "Me too," he said. "I'm happy I'm back. I don't hate this as much as I pretend."

See? Hard to describe, but there was a side to Jason that you could like. You liked him (shamefully) when he was giving someone else a hard time, and you liked him (with justification) when he said he was sorry. Anyway, all very, very hard to explain; especially, I think, if you're his younger brother.

9 ANYWAY, SINCE it came up in therapy, I should tell you more about my band, KISS FOREVER. It kind of took off during that fall, and since it ultimately relates to the story I'm telling, you'll need to know a little more about it.

The founder and leader of KISS FOREVER was a guy named Jim Walters. He was thirty-six, lived with his mother and four cats, and worked at an organic restaurant and juice bar during the day. He was a vegetarian of extreme conviction and talked endlessly about the dangers—to both body and soul—of eating meat. This did not, however, prevent him from spitting fake blood all over himself during KISS FOREVER shows. It was a contradiction, but because it was a contradiction, it explained some of his passion for KISS.

"We all have a kind of wildness in our hearts," he once told me. "A band like KISS FOREVER lets us visit our wild side through the imagination, without having to visit it in reality. We get to explore the feelings without the consequences."

Frankly, such explanations always left me feeling a bit unsatisfied. After all, I lived with a guy who visited the wildness in his heart almost every day, and KISS FOREVER hardly seemed like a solution. On the other hand, to see Jim onstage, I was happy he had the band. He behaved like such a lunatic that I'd hate to imagine what he'd be like without this imaginary outlet. He'd definitely be eating lots of meat.

Anyway, Jim played bass and was lead singer, which made him Gene Simmons in the band. He even had a pretty long tongue, although it was nothing compared to Gene Simmons's magnificent organ. If you ever get the chance, check out Gene's tongue in a KISS fan book at the library or in a bookstore. It's really incredible. Really.

The one other thing I should say is that Jim owned the band van, the vehicle we carted our stuff around in. This is also important.

Member number two was a guy named Philip Hansen. He and Jim had been best friends since they were juniors in high school and had shared their love of KISS for nearly twenty years. Philip actually had a pretty good job. He was a paralegal (or a lawyer's assistant), which is a good job for a band guy. He had pretty regular hours, he could take time off when he needed it, and he had a decent income, so he wasn't stressed all the time. Philip loved KISS for all the reasons Jim loved KISS, although there was something a little less spiritual about his love. He bought into all the wild-side talk. But I think Philip loved KISS and being in KISS FOREVER because he loved having roomfuls of women screaming at him. In some ways Philip embodied the true spirit of KISS. As far as I can tell from the interviews of KISS members, most of them became performers to meet women. This is definitely true for Philip. Philip, by the way, played drums. This made him Peter Criss in the band.

The last member was a guy named Mitch Obermeyer. Mitch did something with computers by day, and in his free time he tried to think up different ways to make himself look cool. Frankly, I liked Mitch very little, and he liked me even less. Jim and Philip started the band and recruited me and Mitch at about the same time. Mitch played rhythm guitar, while I played lead. There are all sorts of arguments about whether or not lead has more status than rhythm. Maybe for musicians lead does not. But I will make one point: lead guitar gets the crowd screaming like nothing else. Rhythm guitar can't compete.

The one thing I will say for Mitch is that he loved playing guitar, and when we had a good night, he was all smiles after the show. And if I played really well, he'd tell me so. It was always seeing him the next day or at practice that he'd act like a jerk again, barely even coming up with a "wussup" to greet me. I think he didn't like the fact that I was sixteen. He said as much. On several occasions he said things like, "When are we going to ditch the kid?" Fortunately, the other guys liked me. I was like their mascot. They enjoyed initiating me into the world of KISS fanaticism. And I was good, which is really why a bunch of thirty-somethings wanted to play with me. I was pretty good. Better than some of their other options, I think.

Anyway, we had formed the previous winter, and spent that spring and summer (the summer Jason was sent away) learning songs and playing wherever we could. It was kind of a fun time. We worked on our costumes (my mom especially), experimented with makeup (I am ashamed to say), and developed some of our onstage dance moves (stunning). We practiced in Jim's mother's garage, and it was fun getting to know the other band members, freaks though they were. I also loved playing guitar, although the KISS music could sometimes get annoying after a while.

Playing small clubs and bars over the summer had been fun because people didn't expect too much. You could blow a lead and people wouldn't care. Or they wouldn't even know. Sometimes it was pretty thankless. We once played at a bar called The Green Burn, which was a German techno place where people were absolutely appalled by our music. Almost as appalled as I was. This was the only time we were actually booed. We also played a few little roadhouses in northern Illinois where people didn't seem to notice us one way or another.

The best place we played was a little basement joint called the Flame. It was really just a room—no decorations to speak of. The nice thing was that we became regulars. We played about once every two weeks from May onward. It got our name out, and people started coming by regularly to see us.

And by the time September rolled around, our status shot way up, because we were booked at a place called the Shoreline, which was a huge club near the lake. The owner was a former pro-football player from way back named Joe Curtis, and he could not have been more revolted by our music. But we were drawing big audiences at the Flame, so he decided to book us. Club owners will tell you that they're all about promoting new music. But they're also all about making money, and if you've got people who will come to hear you, then you're worth booking.

"I don't see why anyone likes this stuff," Joe said when we first met with him.

"This is art, man," Jim said. "That's why they like it." But he kind of smiled when he said this. I think he was kind of amused by Joe.

"Well, they do like it," Joe replied. "That's for sure. But it's sure a mystery to me. Frankly, I don't understand why people like anything that comes out these days. I like swing, big band. Old-fashioned dance music. You guys like that?"

We all shrugged our shoulders. The answer was definitely no, but no one wanted to offend him.

"That's what I thought. Well, there's no money in it, so it doesn't really matter. But the minute it comes back, this place is changing its look. Until then, I'd love to have you guys come play here."

So that was good news. We agreed to play in early September, about the time I had to head back to school. The gig was quite a step up. It was a big club, we could charge twenty bucks a ticket, and they advertised on the radio.

The show was also helpful for reasons other than status and money. First of all, it was the only time that all of our now fairly regular fans could assemble in one place. Usually we were playing in cramped bars to a small portion of our regular audience. At the Shoreline, not only could everyone fit, but everyone came because, after all, it was a big show at the Shoreline.

Second, because the place filled up, we realized that we had the ability to draw new fans. KISS tribute bands were apparently in, and people who had only just heard of us were willing to show up and fork over twenty bucks.

Third, the gig was a sort of final exam for everything we had been working on that summer. It tested our costumes, our makeup, our dance moves, our blood-spitting skills, to say nothing of our musical abilities. And we worked hard for this exam. We practiced every day for two weeks before that show.

Finally, and most important (I mean it: of pivotal importance), I got a taste of what it is like to play screaming guitar leads in front of hundreds of delirious fans. Trust me—there's nothing like it. Even when you're a fake and you're not sure you like what you're playing. That night, we played two sets of our best-rehearsed KISS songs and then a three-song encore, where I belted out guitar licks like I never had before. I played so well mostly because I was taken up with the spirit of the whole thing. Really. A crowd like the one at the Shoreline that night makes you a million times better. It's easy to be creative when there are all sorts of people screaming your name. Of course, they weren't actually screaming my name. They were screaming "Ace," the name of the guy I impersonate. But one way or another, the fans were screaming for me.

So it was all a big success, and afterward, Joe came backstage to let us know how happy he was.

"You really pulled them in tonight," he said. "I mean it. This was a big night."

We were all sweating and exhausted, but it was nice to get that kind of praise, especially from an ex–football player.

"Call me tomorrow," he said, "and we'll see when we can schedule you again."

10

THE NIGHT I got home from the Shoreline gig was the first time Jason had been allowed out for the evening, and he had blown it. He was supposed to be back by 9:00, but he wasn't in till 9:30. For most kids, half an hour isn't that big of a deal, and 9:30 is still pretty early. But when you're a guy like Jason, any rule breaking counts against you.

I actually got home much later than that. After the show, we had to pack up our gear. Then we hung around the dressing room for a while, relaxing and talking about the performance. I didn't get back to my house until 1:00 A.M. I found Jason fuming in front of the television.

"Hey," I said as I walked through the door.

"Get lost," he replied.

"Get in trouble tonight?"

"Came home half an hour late. Mom and Dad went crazy." Jason paused for a second. "How come you get to stay out so late? I don't remember being allowed to come home after one when I was sixteen."

"I was working."

"Playing guitar isn't working," Jason said.

"I get paid."

"Maybe so. But it's still not work."

I paused for a second. "So did Mom and Dad ground you?"

"I'm already completely grounded. They just grounded me worse. I don't think I'm going to be allowed out again for a while."

"Maybe they'll soften up in a couple of days."

"I hope so."

Jason paused for a second, and then turned his eyes back to the TV. He was watching a black-and-white movie about World War II. I looked at the TV for a minute and then turned and headed toward the stairs.

Then Jason started talking again.

"So, did you play well tonight?" he asked, looking back at me.

I stopped again. "Pretty well," I said.

"That's what I figured you'd say. I wonder if it's the truth."

"It's the truth," I said. "Trust me. I was probably even better than Ace."

Jason just smiled at me and then again looked back to the TV.

"Good night," he said.

"Good night," I replied.

So I guess Jason and I didn't fight all the time. We were never buds. But we didn't fight all the time. That was actually one of the good things about my sister, Olivia. Lots of times she could make things easier between Jason and me. Jason wasn't a bully around Olivia at all, and he was even kind of sweet sometimes, if you can imagine that.

For instance, about two weeks after Jason had gotten back from juvie, he, Olivia, and I were all sitting in front of the TV when Olivia asked Jason what "juvie camp" had been like.

"Did you get locked up in a cell?" Olivia asked.

"No, no cell," Jason said. "We were locked up, but in a big dormitory with lots of other guys. It wasn't really like jail. We weren't allowed to run around. But it wasn't like jail."

"What did you do all day?"

"School. Classes. Wood shop. Exercise. That kind of thing."

"Did you like it?"

"It was all right. Wasn't as bad as you'd think. But it wasn't that much fun, either. It was a lot like summer school, but I didn't get to go home at the end of the day. Would have been better if you'd been there with me." Jason smiled at this point and softly placed his index finger on Olivia's nose.

Now, again, let me point out that this kind of interaction between Olivia and Jason was completely unique. That is, I never got to hang out with him that way, except for this kind of situation— when Olivia was around and they were having fun together. In fact, I was so taken up by my brother's nonchalant and lighthearted answers to Olivia's questions that I even took a shot at asking him something. I asked him what the food was like. Normally, this kind of curiosity would have made Jason punch me in the stomach. With Olivia around, he was different.

"As bad as you can imagine food being," he replied.

"Like, what did you have?" I asked.

"Half the time, you didn't even know. And when you did know, you wished you didn't. Pretty much everything looked like meat loaf."

"Yuk," Olivia said. "I hate meat loaf. I'd rather starve to death."

Jason kind of smiled at this. "You get used to it," Jason said, and then he suddenly grabbed Olivia and started tickling her. Just lightly, but she started laughing and screaming and then tried to tickle Jason back. This went on for a few minutes before they tired themselves out and fell back on the couch, laughing and breathing hard.

I have to say that seeing Jason with Olivia was always an eye-opener for me. An important eye-opener. It reminded me that there was a human side to him. I couldn't imagine joking around with him like that. That's why it was important for me to see it. Reminded me that Jason was more than just a brute who pushed me around.

Kind of made me sad actually. Can't say why. Maybe it was just that I felt a little left out. But when Jason, Olivia, and I hung out together, I still always felt pretty good. Even if Jason and I weren't the ones palling around, it still made me feel good.

| 11 | **ANYWAY,** like I said, we brought in good money to the Shoreline, so Joe decided to book us again, three weeks

later. We also quickly got a gig at another pretty big club downtown, called Frog Bar. All this was good news. These shows paid more money and drew way more fans.

Because things with the band were heating up, I also made a pretty radical decision that fall. I decided not to go out for fall soccer. It actually wasn't such a big decision. I was never really a great soccer player. But a man wants to hold on to some kind of hopes of being an athlete. Giving up soccer was my way of finally admitting that being an athlete was not in the cards for me. It was kind of strange. But I really didn't have much of a choice. It was either give up soccer or miss KISS FOREVER practices. Since it was very unlikely that I'd get rich and famous as a soccer player, KISS FOREVER won the battle.

The band usually practiced in the early evening. Like I said, we met at Jim's house and played in his garage. The first practice after the Shoreline gig was pretty fun. We were all pumped up from our raging success and our practice was almost as good as the show.

Truthfully, it was kind of weird sometimes to be hanging out with dudes in their thirties. Sometimes I wasn't sure if they gave me enough credit. Other times I thought they were ignoring my input when they were scheming about the band. But after the Shoreline gig, I really felt like I was on equal footing. They seemed really happy to see me when I showed up. Even Mitch had praise for my guitar playing.

"Incredible show," he said, the first practice after the Shoreline gig. "I mean it. You were on fire."

"Thanks," I said.

"Really. You were probably better than Ace."

"Hey," Jim interrupted. "He was great. But watch what you say about Ace. Let's not get carried away." One of Jim's rules about the band was that we were never, ever to speak of KISS with anything less than the utmost respect. "But you were great out there," Jim added again. "Very impressive."

We took it easy that session. We talked about the gig, song by song. Jim took notes and recorded any comments we made. Then we played a few songs that we thought we could improve on. It felt really productive.

It was one of the first fall evenings of the year. The temperature had dropped the night before and it was freezing outside, so we rigged the garage with portable heaters. The toasty garage kind of mirrored how I was feeling. As goofy as KISS FOREVER was, there was something about it that seemed to be working, and that felt pretty good. I can tell you that it felt better than soccer practice, where I always felt a little slower and clumsier than everyone else.

12

OBVIOUSLY one of the other things that happened that fall was that I returned to school. As a junior, as I think I mentioned.

School has always come pretty easy for me. I've never worked that hard, so it's not like I got straight As. But I studied, did my homework, and got grades worthy of a reasonably smart, college-bound young man. My struggles in school came in the department of women, which I think I've mentioned, and the chief struggle in this regard came with a girl named Amanda.

Amanda was also a junior, and unfortunately, I was not the only one to notice her. There were quite a few guys who wanted to go out with her as well. I will admit (because I am a humble man) that several of these guys were perhaps slightly more handsome than I. Still, that was who I wanted to go out with, and, probably because she was so nice, I always felt like I had some kind of chance.

Amanda had kind of a tomboy thing going. She was tall, strong, really tan, and always wore beat-up jeans and an oversized T-shirt or sweater. She had dark eyes and dark hair, and seemed to be friends with absolutely everyone in the school. She also seemed to go through a lot of boyfriends (boyfriends that were not me). But the good side of that was that no one really ever seemed to make her happy—so, a good opportunity for me to jump in, I thought.

And since we're on the subject of my social world, I also had two close friends at school, and about eight million other friends that I knew, said hi to in the halls, etc., but that I wasn't tight with.

My two close friends were named Fitz and Anthony. See below:

Fitz (short for James Albert Fitzhugh): a kind-hearted and quick-witted guy, described earlier as the kid who had his tooth knocked out by Jason after the Monopoly game. Fitz was short, thin, and had a talent for pissing off guys bigger than him. My brother was, in fact, only one of many guys who beat Fitz to a pulp. Actually, most people liked Fitz, so he wasn't always being beaten up. All the same, we'd usually have to peel him off the school parking lot at least once a semester. Fitz was also a grade hound and everything in his life was oriented around getting As. He planned to go to Harvard, become an investment banker, and be extremely rich. "What else would I do?" he said.

Anthony: Of the three of us, Anthony went over best with women. He was a good athlete (was a receiver on the football team); had huge blue eyes (which girls apparently like); and he was a kind, warm guy (a grossly exaggerated characteristic when ladies were around). Anthony moved to town in seventh grade and Fitz and I adopted him as a friend. He came from California, which meant that he had all sorts of bizarre affectations and speech patterns. Fitz and I quickly helped him understand the correct way a man ought to behave in the Chicago area. One big advantage to being friends with Anthony was that he was really rich and really spoiled. That is, he had everything he wanted and more. Now, wealth is no reason to befriend someone. But if a friend happens to be rich, I say you should enjoy the spoils as much as possible. Fitz and I tried to go over to Anthony's house whenever possible to swim in his pool, watch his plasma TV, and lounge around his overstocked kitchen.

Anyway, anytime I went to a party or a dance, I was usually hanging out with those two guys. And I was usually trying to get Amanda to hang out with us as well—when we appeared at the same party or dance or sports event. She was always nice. She'd always stop and say hi to us. Still, never exactly what I was looking for.

The longest conversation I had with Amanda that September was actually at a school dance. I went with Fitz and Anthony, and my brother, Jason, tagged along, which I went along with because he and my mother suggested it—a kind of easy way for my brother to be social without hanging out with criminals.

Fitz and Anthony, of course, were scared out of their minds by Jason, although they all managed to be civil to each other at public events. They could even occasionally talk to each other, as they did that evening when we first arrived and the subject of the Chicago Bulls came up. The three of them started debating the team's prospects, while I decided to slip away to find Amanda. It took a couple of passes around the darkened school gym, but I eventually spotted her.

"What's up, Amanda," I said, as I sidled up next to her at the huge buffet of potato chips and soda.

"Hey, Will," she said. "Having a good time?"

"Yep," I said.

"That's good," she said.

"Are you having a good time?"

"Yes. I am."

"Good. Me too." I paused for a few moments. "Did you like the last dance we had?"

"Yep. Did you?"

"Sure did. A great dance."

"It was fun."

"Yep. Very fun."

Anyway, I could continue to recount more of our ridiculous discussion, but it never really went beyond this kind of idiotic chatter. The only significant thing happened a few minutes into our talk, when my brother arrived. Why, you might ask, did he come over to us? Because, as usual, he had the urge to humiliate me. I was standing there innocently talking with Amanda about how we both liked school dances, when he came up behind me, put me in a headlock, messed up my hair, told

Amanda that she should escape while she had the chance, and then slapped me on the face a few times. At first Amanda just stood there without much of an idea of what to do. I only caught glimpses of her facial expression because, after all, I was trapped in a headlock. She wasn't laughing, which was good, but she definitely looked confused. Finally she just said, "Well, I'll leave you guys to it. Have fun." And then she walked off.

After she was gone, my brother finally let me up. Needless to say, I was furious.

"Why the hell did you do that?" I yelled.

"I was just trying to put you in your place," he responded, laughing. "I don't want you to get conceited. You're not really a rock star yet." And then he smiled at me like the whole thing was funny, like he had just done something really funny.

I just looked back at him, not smiling, trying to give him a look that would show him how pissed off I was. Finally I said, "It's getting close to your curfew, Jason. Maybe you'd better get your coat and go home to Mom."

Jason's face dropped and I thought he was going to hit me. I think under different circumstances he would have—right in the nose. But if he got into a fight at a school dance, he'd be history, and he knew it. Instead he just clenched his fists and walked away. Funny. I felt pretty bad all of a sudden. I didn't think that I should feel bad for saying what I said. I mean, it wasn't too cool of him to push me around in front of Amanda. Still, I felt bad. And I felt even worse about five minutes later when Jason came up to Fitz, Anthony, and me, wearing his coat.

"I'm taking off, men," he said. "Heading home."

"Why so early?" Anthony asked.

"Bored, I guess," he replied. "I'm missing some good TV."

I paused for a second, and I wanted to tell him to stay. But the fact is that I was also still a little pissed. I guess it's understandable. All the same, looking back on it, I wish that I'd asked him to hang out a little while longer.

13

LIKE I MENTIONED, one of the things that kept my parents busy was carting my sister Olivia around to all her dance practices. I may be biased, but she was pretty good. There were a couple of kids who were better—I guess I can admit that—but Olivia was definitely in the top 20 percent. Probably not going to be her job when she got older, but it definitely landed her good roles in the various productions around town. My parents were never pushy with Olivia (or me or Jason, for that matter). They encouraged us, but they were never like some parents who spend all their time trying to get their kids to be child geniuses. So it's not like they were pushing Olivia into anything. She was just a good dancer. And she loved it.

Her favorite kind of dance was ballet, and that fall she had made the decision to cut out some of her other dance classes to add more ballet to her schedule. She put away her tap shoes, gave up "body art" classes at the Chicago Fine Art Center, and started going to ballet four times a week. She also got a role in a kind of regional production of *Swan Lake* (a famous ballet, if you've never heard of it), and a lot of that fall was spent taking her to rehearsals at a small theater in the next town over.

Since my mom didn't work, she usually drove Olivia to ballet. But every so often that fall, I was asked to fill in. I always liked doing this, mostly because it gave me a chance to impart some of my wisdom to Olivia. I'd tell her about life, the world, her future. She'd say things like, "Will you please leave me alone," or "Why are you always lecturing me?"

She was a funny kid. And all that sarcasm—I taught her every bit of it.

Two of the common themes I tried to address with my sister were the evils of vanity and the importance of honesty and hard work. A vanity that used to bother me was Olivia's love of fancy dresses. It seemed so contrary to her love of ballet. Admittedly, ballet is kind of pointless (like playing guitar, I guess), but at least there's real athletic activity involved. My sister's love of pretty, frilly dresses seemed absurd when matched to her fairly impressive physical power when she was dancing, and the costumes got more elaborate with *Swan Lake.* I once even gave Olivia a long lecture regarding this issue, saying that ballet was a noble art form, but also a little superficial.

"Like, why do you have to wear such ridiculous outfits?" I said.

"You dress up like a monster and spit blood when you perform," she replied.

"Fine. But I know the way I dress is ridiculous."

"And the fact that you know you're ridiculous makes you a better person?"

"Exactly."

One of the real problems with Olivia's strange costumes was that she hated to wear her seat belt in the car, and I was a big believer in safety. She claimed that the seat belt ruined her ballet dresses. I insisted that a dress was no reason to act recklessly.

"I don't care if you rip that outfit to shreds," I'd say. "You are wearing a seat belt when I'm driving this car."

"No way."

"Yes way."

"No way. Forget it. No seat belt."

"Seat belt. This instant. Right now."

"No way."

"Yes way."

Often this sort of argument would last for the whole car trip. And even if I pinned her down and

45

put the seat belt on her myself, she'd always undo it as soon as I returned to my seat.

But all this was fun. Olivia was fun to spend time with. And like I've already said, even Jason thought this. Jason had similar good times with her. But I think it's worth saying that it was more than fun. Jason really cared about Olivia, and I think she could make him feel pretty guilty about the crap he pulled.

I remember one night (maybe a year before that fall) Jason got brought home by the cops for breaking a window at a local grade school. He said it was an accident, which might actually be true, but he was climbing around on the roof and had a friend's BB gun with him, so it wasn't like he was serving ice cream to needy children.

But for some reason Jason was in a pissy mood that night and wasn't really interested in getting lectures from anyone. The cops told him he was going to have to appear in court, and that BB guns were "more dangerous than you'd think," and even that the Kensington taxpayers weren't going to foot the bill for his vandalism.

Jason considered all this, very carefully it seemed, and then took the opportunity to tell the police officers to "go screw yourselves," igniting a fairly wild scene involving both my parents desperately apologizing to the cops at the same time that they were screaming their heads off at Jason. All rough, but not that cataclysmic, at first. The thing was that my little sister was there, standing kind of in the background of this whole scene, and in the next second, she was crying hysterically. My parents were pretty protective of her, and did their best to keep her away from Jason's drama. But more importantly, Jason was protective of her, and when she started crying, he took it harder than any of us. She just kept screaming, "Why are you fighting? Why are you fighting?" The whole time, tears were streaming down her face. Jason still had his tough-guy act going, and he was still glaring at the cops, but when my parents started screaming even more, now furious with Jason for causing all of this, he just suddenly went berserk and pushed my father into a wall. It was kind of stunning—just a notch up from anything he'd done before—but all he could say (or scream in a totally garbled voice) was that everyone was upsetting Olivia and he wasn't going to let that happen. Not atypical logic for Jason.

At any rate, the now slightly confused cops stood around to make sure no one threw any punches, but Jason quickly ran up the stairs (still yelling that he hadn't done anything wrong), and about this point, the cops decided that this had all become more of a "family matter." In the middle of all the screaming, they politely told my parents that Jason would be receiving paperwork in the mail, and then they left.

Jason didn't resurface again that night, and in the meantime my now very concerned parents talked about what was next. I know this because I came out of my room later that night to get something to eat, and on the stairs, on my way down to the kitchen, I overheard them discussing the situation. It was kind of late, and they were still up, and still talking about the whole thing. Mostly they were talking about how to explain all this to Olivia. But they were stumped by the whole thing, and (probably for the thousandth time) they were talking about what they could do to straighten out Jason. I heard the phrase "Military Academy" several times. And I also heard the term "medication" more than once, which was a constant issue. I know that my brother took pills—every kind, as far as I could tell, for every kind of diagnosis. Ritalin, Prozac, Zyprexa, Wellbutrin, you name it. All the things people take to calm themselves down or pick themselves up or get to sleep or make themselves study harder. This is not really something that was discussed much with me, and definitely not with Olivia. It was hardly any of our business. But my parents administered the pills, knowing that Jason wasn't going to take them on his own, and it was hardly something we could avoid noticing. Anyway, like I said, this was something my parents were talking about.

"I mean, I just hate it all," my mother said. "They're clearly not working and I just hate pumping him full of chemicals. And, maybe selfishly, they make me feel like such a failure. I mean, what kind of mother am I?"

"You're a good mother," my father replied. "And Jason's not all bad. He's got a heart. He does. We've seen that side to him. We haven't totally failed. He's just got a decision-making problem. He gets caught up in things before he knows what's going on."

"I don't know," my mother said. "I just feel so guilty, and I feel like this problem is going to get worse and going to hurt everybody. I don't want Olivia to go through that again." Pause. "But maybe it was good for Jason to see all that—to see the pain he can cause other people."

There was another pause. Then finally my father said, "Maybe. Maybe. But I hate to see either of them that upset."

Funny. My dad's compassion suddenly seemed like some kind of denial. Still, I also think my dad's assessment of Jason was mostly right, especially about Jason's decision-making abilities. Strange, but over the years, a thing that always marked his delinquency was his own surprise. Like, after he had finished lighting the fire or spray-painting his name on the wall or punching the kid in the face, he was more surprised than anyone else, like he had no idea what was happening, to say nothing of thinking he was the cause of the problem.

Whatever. I know in this kind of story, there's supposed to be some kind of firm decision—packing the boy off to military school, shooting him up with some kind of new medication, calling out the psychologists. But everyone was stumped. My parents' conversation didn't even really end. My father said, "I just don't know what to do. We have to keep thinking about this."

But there was no more talk after that. The next thing I heard was my mom walking around in the kitchen, and I decided I'd better stop hiding out on the stairs. In the next second, I was standing at the fridge, looking at a stack of yogurts, and talking to my mother about an upcoming math test.

14   SO, KISS FOREVER's gig at Frog Bar came at the end of September. It was as big a deal as the Shoreline show, so we practiced pretty hard for it.

My parents were pretty cool about my being in the band. After all, it's not exactly a parent's dream for his or her son to be jumping around onstage in demonic makeup, with blood dripping out of his mouth. The one thing that sometimes bothered my mom was how much time it took. Like I said, I was a pretty good student, and when my mom asked me how classes were going, I could always produce tests and papers with As and Bs to keep her satisfied. But when it came to time away from the family, especially dinner, she'd get pretty irritable. Occasionally, she'd even put her foot down, like in the week before the Frog Bar gig.

I had been spending all my time in Jim's garage, playing with the band. On Wednesday I came home at about 5:00 P.M. to have a quick sandwich before I headed back to the garage. As I was getting out the peanut butter and bread, my mom intercepted me.

"I want you to eat at home tonight," she said.

"No can do," I replied. "Big practice. Fame and fortune hang in the balance. Have to practice, practice, practice."

"Let me say that again. I want you to eat at home tonight. I also want you to stay in afterward. We rented a movie and I want you to be around for it."

I was about to decline her invitation again, but when I saw her face, I realized that I couldn't joke my way out of it. So I turned to begging, which sometimes worked.

"Mom. You don't understand. I've got to practice. We have a really important show this weekend."

"At Frog Bar. Yes, I've heard. Don't care. You have to stay in tonight. Your family misses you, Will."

"But the guys in the band will kill me. I mean it. They think it's bad enough that they play with a sixteen-year-old. If they find out I can't practice because my mom won't let me, I'm finished."

"Go wash your hands. I want you to help me make a salad."

I started to plead again, but my mother gave me another look to suggest that I shouldn't push my luck, and I knew that my mom was not above asserting her control over me by grounding me the night of the Frog Bar show. It was like a police state at my house. My mom was usually pretty nice to me, but she would accept no challenge to her authority.

"Hang on," I sighed. "I need to call Jim to tell him I won't be there tonight."

Fortunately, Jim was pretty cool about the whole thing. He said that he and the other members could get by without me if I promised to put in extra time the next day. So I helped my mom with dinner instead of going to practice, and it actually wasn't all that bad. My mom was pretty cool. She's actually the person who got me into guitar. I was about seven when my parents decided it might be nice for me to start learning to play an instrument. My dad had all sorts of ridiculous ideas of me becoming a classical musician, and only wanted me to play weird instruments like the bassoon or the French horn. My mom objected, saying that I'd be better off playing an instrument that matched the music I'd be listening to. She said that if I was interested in the music, I'd practice more. And she was right. The lessons I took at first were pretty basic, and I didn't get very far. But by about age eleven, I figured out that I could play the music that I was listening to on the radio. At that point, I really improved. I played for at least an hour every day. Always on my own, without my parents bugging me.

The other thing is that my mom actually plays guitar. She's all right. Not bad, but not great. She plays a different kind of guitar. She was something of a hippie when she was younger, and plays folk music on an acoustic guitar. Anyway, needless to say, I wanted nothing to do with that kind of music. Still, it was good to have someone around to give me pointers.

And here's a pretty strange fact (something that always blows my mind): my mother's favorite kind of music was popular about the same time KISS started to get popular. How the American cultural scene in the seventies produced two such opposite musical styles is one of the world's great mysteries. Neither my mother nor I could ever figure that one out.

| 15 | **THE OWNER** of Frog Bar was an old guy named Jack Farr, who dressed like he was in a boy band and acted |

like it too. He was a booster and an organizer around Chicago and had actually hosted the battle of the bands where Jim first saw me play. My band didn't win, but I did pretty well, and Jack even nodded at me as we left the stage. Still, when we showed up the afternoon of the gig to check out the location and to adjust the sound system, he didn't seem to recognize me. All he did was smile at us and tell us how happy he was to have us there.

"I love you guys," he said. "This KISS thing is great. Kids love it. I'm really happy you're here."

"We're happy to be here," Jim said.

"Anything you need, you come to me. Just ask for Jackie, and I'll hook you up."

"Got it," Jim said.

At about this point, another guy approached us. "I've got to run take care of some things," Jack said. "So let me introduce you to my club manager. This is Erik. He loves you guys too. He'll be helping you set up."

"Hey," Erik said, and then shook our hands.

"Just call my name if you need something," Jack said, and then started to head off. But just as he turned, he looked over at me and said, "How's it going, sport? Left your old band, eh?"

"Yeah," I said. "We broke up."

"Well you landed on your feet, kid. This is a great act." Then he smiled again and headed toward his office at the back of the club.

It was actually kind of nice to be recognized, and as I turned to look at the other guys, I noticed that Jim was kind of looking at me and smiling. Jim was also at the battle of the bands that night, and, as I've mentioned, that was when he first approached me about being in KISS FOREVER. I had been in a band that did your standard rock covers—Led Zeppelin, the Who, Rolling Stones,

Doors, etc. Songs I love, but nothing too far out. Also good songs to impress a lover of heavy metal. If you can lead on a Zeppelin tune, you can definitely lead on KISS songs. Anyway, I had been packing up my amp when Jim walked up and introduced himself.

"Dude, you are one righteous guitar player," he said.

"Thanks," I replied, and then, at a loss for what else to say, added, "I think you're righteous too."

"No, I mean it. You were smoking out there. What's your name?"

"Will."

"Will, I'm Jim. Jim Walters." Jim paused for a second while he stroked his chin. Finally he started talking again.

"Listen," he said. "I've got a little project brewing that you might be interested in. Might not be your cup of tea musically, but it would be great experience and you could probably make a little cash."

"I like cash," I replied.

"How old are you?"

"Fifteen."

This made Jim pause a little longer. "Will you have time to practice? This act is going to demand lots of practicing."

"For cash, I can practice all you want."

"Well, greed is the sign of a good musician. What's your phone number? I'll give you a call tomorrow. Maybe we can meet for coffee to discuss the project."

I gave Jim my phone number, and by the following week, I had agreed to join the band. I have to admit, I joined on a lark. But the whole thing was so ridiculous that I couldn't say no to it. What did I have to lose? The answer to this question was, my dignity. Still, it was worth it. And not just because I got paid.

Anyway, after Jack-the-owner left, Erik-the-club-manager took us to the sound board and started going over the equipment with us. I kind of drifted off at this point. The other guys in the band totally loved electronics and sound equipment, so I usually let them handle everything. I just looked around and tried to get a feel for the place.

Frog Bar was huge. It had two stories, the lower story being where we were going to play. The downstairs was the size of a small warehouse, and had lights and strange glass sculptures on all the walls. Seeing it with all the lights on was kind of strange. It was like looking at an X-ray of someone. Everything that was normally hidden—the wiring, the seams, the wall joints, the service exits, etc.— was visible. Of course, I had never seen it when the lights were dimmed either. I was, after all, underage, and not really allowed into the club as a customer. (That was one of the fun things about playing with KISS FOREVER, I guess. Getting to see things a junior in high school doesn't normally get to see. But I'll say more on this subject in a bit.) Anyway, with all the lights on, it didn't seem like such a happening joint. But when we went back later that night, when things got going, the place was pretty incredible.

We arrived at about 7:00 on the evening of the show. The lights were just being dimmed. We were due on at 9:00. They said they hoped we could stretch the concert out till midnight and that we could take two long breaks if we wanted.

The dressing room was actually pretty nice. It had a couple of couches and about eight padded chairs set in front of big mirrors. The mirror thing was important. We had lots of makeup work to do. And it was a pleasure to dress up like Ace Frehley in these surroundings. I had done it in a cramped men's room before. Trust me—that sucks.

We were ready to go on at 9:00, but Jim decided to make the audience wait for another twenty minutes.

"Helps build the anticipation," he said as we were pacing around the dressing room.

Finally, at 9:20, we headed out, and the crowd was, indeed, riled up. They started cheering as soon as they spotted us, although, I will point out again, no one cheered for us or for KISS FOREVER. They cheered for KISS and for Gene Simmons and Ace Frehley and Peter Criss and Paul Stanley. You might imagine that accepting someone else's applause wouldn't be that satisfying. But when you're standing in front of hundreds of screaming and clapping people, it's hard not to feel great. The truth is, a man will take any applause he can get. And in some ways they were cheering for us.

Anyway, I won't bore you with a complete set list. I will say that we opened with the KISS standard "Christine Sixteen" to deafening applause, and we ended the evening with "Detroit Rock City." I may be wrong about this, but it seemed that most of the audience was in tears over Jim's beautiful voice and my heart-straining leads. Actually, to tell the truth, I'm pretty sure I'm wrong about this. But the KISS illusion was as much for us as it was for the audience. So I choose to believe.

16 **IT'S FUNNY,** but when you're telling a story, the parts that seem like they'd be the easiest are usually the hardest. And vice versa. For instance, if I'm sitting around with friends, I can make a pretty boring moment seem pretty interesting. I can talk about the way Amanda brushed by me in biology class, or the way I felt during a snowstorm, or how terrible the school's beef stew is. It's the bigger things that are harder to get right. It seems that for every sentence describing some kind of big event, I also

make an apology for not getting it quite right. It's like telling friends about the funniest thing you've ever seen and then concluding with "I guess you had to be there" because no one seems to be laughing. It's hard to tell good stories, period. And the bigger the story, the harder it gets.

I say all this because I'm not sure I'm getting the performance scenes right. In fact, I hate to even try. The important thing to remember is this: it was a farce and a joke and there are few things that I really liked about KISS, and at the same time, there are few experiences in my life that have been quite as great as impersonating Ace Frehley. Maybe the reason that it's hard to get it right is because it's just so embarrassing. But a screaming crowd has a kind of pull that's unlike anything else. And as you're cruising along in a lead and you manage to pull off a few musical twists and turns that make people gasp, and then the cheering starts, and the older band members nod at you, the universe suddenly seems to be in complete harmony and you seem to be at its center. And if it's really good, if you do this a few times and people cheer like crazy for you, and every time you hit a note it seems like just the right note, the most perfect possible note, the feeling lasts for much longer than the concert. And it's so intense that you don't even know that you're feeling that way until the feeling starts to die down.

It seemed like that at Frog Bar. It seemed like I forgot where I was until I was back in the dressing room taking off my makeup and talking about the night with the other band members. Still, even as the feeling died down, it was pretty intense. My leads had been solid, and the audience seemed to think that my leads were good, and the band members treated me like I was a pretty serious musician. Even Mitch. Even Mitch was acting like this. In the midst of all our chatter, Mitch leaned over and said, "I gotta admit kid. I'm pretty jealous about the way you played tonight. I hate to say it. But it's the truth. You were great."

That was a cool moment. Whatever. I guess you had to be there.

17 SO, AFTER the Frog Bar gig, we got a bunch of offers to play other places. And Frog Bar wanted us to come back in a month. Our act had been tight, but more important, we brought in customers. Paying fans. Can't beat that for impressing people who book bands.

The new work also made us think about making a few changes. Nothing big. But we decided that we might want to hire a few people to help us out at our shows. Roadies.

"We need a sound guy," Jim said as we sat on stools by the workbench in the garage the day after the Frog Bar show. (Basically, a sound guy sits at the back of the show with a big electronic sound board and adjusts all the various speakers and microphones to make sure everything sounds right.)

"The only complaint I have about last night was with Erik's setup," Jim continued. "It wasn't bad. But it could have been better. If we have our own guy monitoring us during our shows, we could sound a lot better and be a lot more consistent. And since we're making some cash, I think now's the time to get someone."

"What we need is bouncers," Mitch said. "And a sound guy. We need a sound guy. But we need bouncers. There were some pretty crazy fans there last night."

"I thought you liked that," Philip said.

"Well, it's true that I like fans. But not ones that want to kill me."

"They wanted to kill you?"

"Well, probably not. But they wanted to grab me and pull at me. A guy could die if there were too many."

"Can you really die if you get grabbed too much?"

"I don't see why not. What if they grabbed my neck? I could suffocate."

"Why would they want to grab your neck?"

"All right, all right, all right," Jim said, trying to bring the conversation back to Earth. "I was actually going to suggest hiring a few guys to carry around our stuff. I'm sure they wouldn't mind if we called them our bodyguards as well."

"Cool," Philip said. "Guys to carry our stuff. I like the sound of that."

"Yeah," Jim said, "but they're not our slaves and we're not getting soft. I just think that the band has grown enough to hire a few people. It's too much for us to load our equipment, play a couple of sets, and then put all our stuff back in the van. I could barely move this morning."

"They'd kind of be like our slaves," Mitch said.

"No, they won't kind of be like our slaves," Jim replied.

"Kind of."

"No. Not even kind of."

"Yes."

"No. They won't be our slaves."

Obviously the band was a little excited by our success the night before.

Anyway, after discussing the possible new employees, we played a few songs for fun and then cut the practice short. We were playing again in a week, but at the Flame, so there wasn't too much pressure. This was good because I had some homework to catch up on. I'd been kind of blowing it off.

When I got home that evening—about 7:00— my family members were all going about their regular business. Dad was reading the paper in the study. Mom sat at her sewing machine, working on a new outfit for Olivia while keeping an eye on a pot roast she was making for dinner. Olivia was prancing around the house, practicing her pirouettes. Jason was lounging in front of the television watching a baseball game.

Happy family. Suburban bliss. After the previous night's show and an evening of fixing makeup and spitting blood, I felt pretty happy to be in the midst of such normal surroundings.

And the family seemed happy to see me. Dad asked me how the show went. "How'd it go, Ace?" he yelled when he saw me walking by the study.

"It was great," I said.

When my mom heard my voice, she called out to me and asked if I needed any repair work on my costume. "I've got the sewing machine on," she said. "Now would be a good time."

"The costume's fine, Mom," I said.

It all just seemed so happy that I kind of got swept up in the moment and did something that was a little out of character, perhaps something I would not have ordinarily had the guts to do. I sat on the couch next to Jason, asked how he was doing, and then asked him if he might like a job with the band.

Jason looked up at me. "Like a roadie?" he said.

"Yeah, like a roadie."

"You want me to be your slave?"

"What's with everyone? A roadie is not a slave. A roadie is a roadie. Anyway, you'd help with the equipment, and watch the stage so fans don't attack us. You'd be more like a bodyguard."

"You have fans attacking you? I don't believe it."

"There are a few. Kind of made the guys nervous."

Jason looked at me, smiled, and shook his head.

I suddenly felt kind of bad. Was this insulting? I wondered, offering my older brother a job? Jason looked back at the television and shook his head again. He changed channels, scratched his chin, changed channels again, and then, after a few minutes, said, "All right."

"All right?" I replied.

"All right," he said again, and then switched back to the baseball game.

18 **THE RESULT** of my kind and generous offer? Family mayhem. Never offer a delinquent brother a job before clearing it with your parents first. Never. You will cause so much trouble and fighting that you won't know what to do. Trust me.

Here's what happened.

We ate dinner at 7:30 that night, which is late for us. It was scheduled then to accommodate my band practice. Nice of them. Still, I wish they had eaten without me.

About five minutes into dinner, Jason announced that he had a new job. My mom and dad looked at each other skeptically. They were also kind of frowning, like this was something they weren't going to like. They were right.

"No sir," my dad said when Jason explained that he was going to be a roadie for KISS FOREVER. "That is absolutely out of the question."

"Why?" Jason said angrily.

"You are not going to be hanging around nightclubs. It's out of the question."

"You let Will hang out in nightclubs."

"He's working," my mother said.

"I'd be working too."

"It's different." At this point, my mother was looking pretty angry.

"Why is it different? Do you really think Will is so much better than me?"

"It has nothing to do with better," my dad said. "You've got a pretty bad track record and you know it. You're just going to have to lay low for a while until we're sure you can behave yourself. It's not an issue of our opinions of you. It's an issue of your past actions."

At this point Jason put down his fork, got up from the table, and walked out of the room.

It was tough on him. No question. And everyone knew it. I was allowed to do pretty much whatever I wanted. Jason was not. And when your younger brother is racing around having fun while you're confined to the house every night, things look pretty bleak and pretty unfair. Still, it was also kind of understandable. Get arrested a bunch of times and people get nervous about what you're going to do next.

At the point that Jason left the table, however, I wasn't worried only about him. I had other problems.

"What were you thinking?" my father said. "You know that Jason's situation isn't going to allow for a job like that right now."

"It seemed like a good idea."

"It was not a good idea," my mother said as she abruptly poured milk into Olivia's empty glass. "Let me clear that up right now."

"I really think it would be fine," I replied. "I'd be there. I could keep an eye on him. I don't think there'd be any problems."

At this statement, my parents really started screaming. Seriously pissed.

"It is not your job to keep an eye on your brother," my mother said. "I'm not crazy about you being in nightclubs, frankly, and as far as I'm concerned, your guitar-playing job is purely probationary. You've got to worry about keeping yourself out of trouble. I mean it. If I ever hear about you stepping out of line at one of those places, you are out of that band immediately."

"What did I do?" I said. "All I did was offer Jason something that I thought would be good for him."

"What's good or not good for Jason is not your concern," my dad snapped.

I didn't know what to say. I just started picking at the potatoes on my plate. We were all silent. Finally, Olivia piped up and said that she wanted to learn to play the guitar. "I want to take guitar lessons," she said.

"Forget it," my parents replied simultaneously.

19

BUT THE TRUTH is that parents are usually more confused than you'd think. They make lots of decisions, but my guess is that they spend a lot of time wondering if they've done the right thing. If they're good parents, they do this. My parents are like that. They're pretty good at acting like they know exactly what they're doing. But they sometimes have a hard time making up their minds about things. Especially important things.

Anyway, the next day my brother came to my parents with a proposal. It was a plan of behavior and rewards. He did it all on his own. Remarkable. He basically said that if he kept his nose clean (perfectly clean: no detentions, scoldings, tardiness, insubordination, mutiny, etc.) for the entire month of October, then he should be allowed to work for KISS FOREVER.

Now, such a plan was not convincing in itself. But my brother knew how to play on my parents' sympathy when he wanted to. He said that he was getting worried about his future, what he'd be doing with himself when he got out of high school. He claimed that it was unlikely he'd get into college, or that he'd do very well if he went. But he said that he could imagine working for a band. Start as a roadie, work with the sound guy occasionally, and then who knew what would be next.

"I need to figure out how to do something," he said to my father and mother in the study. "Or I'll be living here for the rest of my life."

My parents thought it over. They had been down this road before with Jason. He was better at blowing second chances than anyone on the planet. In fact, as a rule, just when you thought he was cleaning up his act, he'd strike again.

On the other hand, just the fact that Jason had come up with such a plan was unusual. And the truth was that he had been doing pretty well since he got back from juvie.

The bottom line, however, was this: Jason was indeed going to graduate at the end of the year, and it was anyone's guess what he was going to do with himself. Working for KISS FOREVER seemed like the beginning of a pretty good direction for him to take. He could handle the work. He was interested in it. And there was a way for him to advance. A lot of music guys never went to college.

So after a few days of thinking, my parents gave in. They drew up a long contract with Jason and made a list of every single infraction that would cost him the job. They said he had a month to prove himself, but they expected all the rules to be followed even after the month had passed.

"Getting the job means perfect behavior for the next month," my dad said. "And I mean perfect."

"I understand," Jason said.

"And keeping the job means the same thing," my dad continued. "You mess up once, you've lost the job. Perfect behavior."

"OK," Jason said.

"I mean perfect."

"OK. Perfect."

"Like, not one rule broken."

"Got it."

"Not one."

"Got it."

So that was settled—or as settled as it was going to be. But at this point, I also had another problem. Probably something I should have already worked out. I had to ask the other band members if it was cool to hire my older brother. Definitely something I should have already done. Definitely.

"No way in hell," Mitch said when I asked them the next day at band practice. "One kid is enough."

"He's strong and he really wants the job," I replied. I wasn't too worried about Mitch's response. I knew that Jim and Philip were the guys I had to sell to.

"You've told us some pretty bad stories about Jason," Philip said. "I trust your judgment, but given the things you've said . . ."

"It's true. He's done some pretty rotten things. But this is a great opportunity for him. He really wants to do this. And as far as I can tell, that's only to our advantage. Might be hard to boss a thirty-year-old around. Will be easier with my brother."

Mitch frowned. "But what if he gets grounded on the night of a big show?"

"If that happens," I said, "I'll personally carry all the stuff."

"I don't know," Mitch replied.

"Look, Mitch," I said, "this is as close a thing to a slave as you're going to get. Hire someone older and you're going to have to show him more respect than I know you want to. Plus, Jason is a big, scary guy. If you want to have someone to keep off all the screaming fans, this is your man."

Mitch looked into the air and considered what I was saying. No way was he going to say yes. It was his role in the band to disapprove of everything. But if he didn't say no, that was half the battle.

After another minute, Jim said, "I think we should hire him."

"It's fine by me," Philip added.

Mitch stood up and walked over to his amp. He began to fiddle with the tone settings.

"So what do you think, Mitch?" Philip finally asked.

"What?"

"I said, 'What do you think?'"

Mitch paused for a moment and then said, "Whatever."

And that was as good as a yes.

20

NOW I HAD to think about one other issue, namely, *what the hell was I doing?* I mean, if anyone was liable to suffer with this situation, it was me. Let's face it, I was an object of enormous aggression and hostility for Jason. It wasn't unlikely that I'd be playing the rest of my shows with dead arms and black eyes. In fact, as I walked home from practice that day, after getting approval from the band, all I could think about was that this was the stupidest idea I'd ever had. Still, a few things came to mind, which are probably instructive at this point.

The first story is from a long time ago, and kind of gets at this strange kind of affection I had for my older brother. I was eight and playing Wiffle ball with a few guys from the neighborhood. Fitz was there. These slightly strange twins who lived down the street were there. And this guy who never combed his hair was there. Just your usual collection of eight- and nine-year-olds all hanging out and playing some kind of sport.

The other person who was there was Jason. He showed up late and demanded to play. Actually, he spent about fifteen minutes telling us what losers we all were. Then he demanded that he be allowed to play. And all he wanted to do was bat. Right away. Fitz was batting at the time, and Jason walked right up to him and took the bat away—it was the sawed-off end of a broom with tape on one end. I was pitching, and I threw a few pitches until Jason said he was bored and that he had another idea. He then started chasing one of the twins around, whacking him on the legs. The twin would run, Jason would catch up, start whacking, the twin would stop, plead for his life, and then start running again. No damage was done. No broken legs. Just stinging. Then Jason came after me. Did the same thing. Chased me, caught me, and whacked my legs. He did it for a while, and then moved on to the next kid.

But here's the strange thing. For some reason, when Jason was whacking the twins and Fitz and the kid with the uncombed hair, Jason kept looking back at me and laughing. He kept looking back at me, catching my eye, smiling, and laughing. It was like I was in on the joke. Sure, he did the same thing to me, but when he was targeting someone else, he was sharing it with me; he was somehow looking for my approval.

And how did I react? What did I do during all of this? I laughed back—I looked back at Jason, hollered with delight, and laughed my head off. And what was strange—what was really strange—was that it wasn't just an act. I really thought it was funny. Was one of the funniest things I'd ever seen, watching Jason chase Fitz around with a stick. And the reason it was funny was because somehow Jason let me in on the joke; he somehow decided that day that I was on his side, that it was me and him, even though he took a shot at whacking me as well.

Anyway, again, I guess I'm just trying to point out that a delinquent older brother has a sort of power over a younger brother, no matter what kind of lunatic he is. I hated all of Jason's crap, but the fact is that I was also hungry for his attention. Can't explain it. Seems ridiculous, in fact, that a thinking man like myself could be the victim of such low desires. But it's true. And I think that's kind of the origins of my offering Jason the job. The fact is (and as I've said already) I always craved some kind of alliance with Jason—some kind of friendship with him. And I think I had just been feeling all happy, and all excited, and suddenly some kind of deep feelings for my brother got the best of my better judgment and I offered him the job. I forgot myself, and gave in to that same primal desire that led me (among other things) to join with my brother in laughing over the twins' getting their legs beaten with a stick.

But I think that incident was on my mind for other reasons as well. At a certain point in Jason's little leg-whacking adventure, the twins and the messy kid and Fitz all decided that the stickball game was over and ran home. About the same time, I headed inside, just in case Jason wanted to come after me again. After a while, the phone rang, and after a few minutes, I heard my mom saying things like, "I'm so sorry," "I'm very surprised to hear that," "Are you sure it was Will too?" When she got off the phone, she came in to the family room to have a little chat with me. Jason was on her list. But I was first.

"So, is everything I heard from Fitz's mother true?" she said.

"It was Jason," I said, which wasn't that far from the truth.

"Fitz's mom seemed to think you were in on it too."

"It was Jason," I said again, which (again) was mostly true.

Then my mom changed strategies. I told you that my parents were entirely democratic about the way they raised us. Even-Steven. Fair to everyone. But the fact was that we were very different kids. So while my parents really did have this solid, unwavering way of regarding us, there were obvious exceptions. And I think these occasions were often points in my life when my parents were slightly afraid that I might drift over to the dark side, that I might somehow become like Jason. I don't like to talk about it that way. I don't like to because I know my parents didn't see things in those terms. They'd look you straight in the eye and tell you they're damn lucky to have Jason in their lives. But the point is that while they may have felt love for Jason, they definitely didn't want me to follow in his footsteps. One delinquent in the family was enough. And this was kind of my mother's message that day. In a roundabout way. She said, "Will, I want you to use your head when you're with Jason. He can get kind of crazy, and I know you know that. But that's not your problem. You're a little more relaxed. So when stuff like what went on today happens, I want you to walk away and come find me."

"It was Jason," I said, for the third time, even though I got her point.

"Well, I'm going to talk to Jason. Don't worry about that. I just want to make sure that you remember to use your head."

Funny, this seems like completely reasonable advice. She could have even been more specific about it. If it were me, I would have said, "Don't be like your crazy brother or you'll end up in jail." But my mom said what she said and then suddenly looked all guilty, like she had said something very, very wrong. And I know that Jason got off easy later that day. He was still sent to his room. Still given a stiff talking-to. But my mom also kept saying things like, "You need to learn when to stop. And you have to remember to think about others' feelings. How would you like to have been beaten up by an older kid?"

Jason just sat there staring off into space. Frankly, I don't think Jason would have minded one bit being beaten up by an older kid, although the older kids in our neighborhood were never stupid enough to pick on him.

Anyway, just in case you've somehow found it in your heart to sympathize with the poor little delinquent, later that night, Jason came into my room, pinned me down, and gave me two dead arms like I've never had before. My arms were so bruised that I could barely move them for the next week. Why did he do this? Jason never honored me with an explanation. I think that pretty much ended any kind of criminal partnership that was unfolding between us. No more shared stickball-bat beatings for us. It was too much for me, and I suffered too much at his hands to develop any real kind of an alliance. But I'll tell you this: I never gave up my strange fascination and affection for my brother. Again, there were a lot of things I resented about the guy. That's true. But there was a side of me that really wanted him to like me, to respect me, to flash me laughing grins as he whacked some kid with a broom handle, like I was in on the joke, like it was he and I together, like Jason and I were best friends out having some fun together. Embarrasses me to say it. I mean, the guy was a bona fide criminal. But it's true. Anyway, possibly that explains why I suddenly (and in a moment of insanity) offered Jason a job with KISS FOREVER.

But there's one more thing. And maybe this is what I'm getting at. I think I was also beginning to feel a kind of extreme guilt. My mother's speech (the one about not following Jason) wasn't the last time that speech would be given to me. It was always delivered with phrases like, "You know how much we love Jason." But there was always also the advice to be careful around him. And I think as I got older, this advice seemed less and less necessary—I had already begun to construct my own wall of defense against Jason. So I wonder if maybe I gave Jason that job not because I wanted his affection but, rather, because I was feeling like I didn't need it anymore. It was kind of like I was throwing him overboard, psychologically at least, like it was finally sinking in that Jason wasn't worth the trouble and that I didn't need his approval, or to be close to him. I don't know. Guilt or not, it's hard to explain. But the fact was that the decision was made, so I was going to have to live with it.

21

SO, THE MONTH of October. Jason's probationary month. A lot happened, although most of it had nothing to do with Jason.

First, we hired a sound guy, which was more expensive than any of us thought. It was a good move, but it meant that we could hire fewer work-horses to carry our stuff around. Actually, it meant we'd have only one: Jason. And that wasn't going to be for another month.

The guy we hired was named Arno, and he was a transplant from Sweden. The man knew every-thing about everything and was the perfect guy to be monitoring our equipment. He was also fairly connected in the Chicago music scene, and he kind of took on the roll of manager as well.

His price? An even cut. So, all proceeds were split five ways instead of four. But since he knew what he was doing and he got us work, he was worth it.

"Trust me guys," he said. "I'll make you more money then I'll cost you. And there's no one who knows and loves the KISS sound like I do."

This was actually true. Believe it or not, plenty of Swedish teenagers grew up listening to KISS, and he was apparently the most enthusiastic fan of all. Shocking really. I guess this explains why America gets a bad rap in so many countries. What do we expect when we're selling them millions of KISS albums?

Anyway, the first show Arno worked on was the second Shoreline gig, and I have to say he did a great job. He didn't carry anything. That was a pain in the ass. But once we were onstage, it was great having a guy watch our backs and keep track of everything. There had been shows when we had to stop everything to readjust amplifiers or plug in connections that had come loose. Not with Arno at the helm.

That night was especially fun for me because I was experimenting with a new lead for a KISS song called "Shock Me," written by Ace Frehley, in fact. It has screaming guitar leads, but I had been working on making them even more screaming. The one I came up with lasted for a full three minutes, and I have to say that the crowd was totally moving by the time I finished. "Ace, Ace, Ace," they were all yelling as I pulled off one lick after another. Funny: on the one hand, KISS seems to be a piss-poor example of American culture; on the other hand, they must have understood something—it's no small feat to get crowds of people to love you. And these people loved me.

Even Arno was impressed. As we were hanging out in the dressing room after the show, he kept saying (in his slightly bizarre Swedish accent), "Dude. Whoa. 'Shock Me.' Dude. Incredible. I mean, dude. Dude!"

It was quite a high point for me having this authentic Swedish KISS fan rave on and on. In fact, Arno was so energized that he insisted we all go out after the show. The guys were tired. I was tired. But we were also kind of pumped up. And it seemed like Arno was going to continue to heap praise on us. It seemed worthwhile to listen to that some more. So we got cleaned up, loaded our stuff in Jim's van, and headed down Lake Shore Drive to a place that Arno said was absolutely the coolest place in Chicago. Was it the coolest place in Chicago? Well, I wish I knew. You see, despite the fact that I was one of the guys, everyone's pal, and a true equal among these older guys, there was one hang-up. While cosmic justice might declare me their equal, the law does not. As we were all walking into the so-called coolest place in Chicago, I felt a big hand on my shoulder and heard, "Not so fast, braces."

"What's wrong?" I said, looking up at the most humongous guy I've ever seen in my entire life.

"What are you, twelve?" he asked.

I didn't even know what to say.

"If you're twelve, you can't go in. If you're not twelve, I'll need to see some ID."

At this point Arno turned and looked at the bouncer. "He's with us. He's a professional guitar player."

Good old Arno. He was connected. He'd get me in.

"The professional guitar player has braces," the bouncer said, pointing to my mouth. "Braces. No way he gets in without ID. Good ID. Absolutely legal, lawful, bona fide ID."

"Look," Arno continued. "I know Charlie, the owner. I'm sure he wouldn't mind. This is the lead guitarist from KISS FOREVER."

"Yeah. Charlie's my boss," the bouncer replied. "I know him too. He is a great guy. Just like I'm sure Braces here is. But no way Charlie would want me to let him in. It's nothing personal. We just don't want to get shut down. Been having some problems with underage drinkers recently."

Arno began to speak again but the bouncer cut him off. "Sorry," he said. Then he looked at me and said, "Sorry guy. Can't do it. I'd like to let you in. I really would. But I just can't."

That sudden kindness seemed completely unfair. It's easier to complain when a bouncer is a big, tough oaf. But when he's suddenly nice, what can you do?

"Don't worry about it," I said. "I would have only wanted a soda anyway." Then I looked at the guys, who were giving me this look like, "We'll leave with you if you want, but we really, really, really want to stay." So I just said, "Listen, I should get home anyway. You guys go ahead. I'll just hop on a bus."

"Are you sure?" Jim said.

"Yeah. No problem. Really. You guys go ahead."

They gave me another look of pity, but they weren't going to ask twice.

"We'll see you tomorrow at practice, okay?" Philip said.

"Yeah. See you tomorrow."

I guess in the end it wasn't so bad. I really did need to get home anyway. My trusting parents wouldn't have been too happy if I had gone to a bar.

That's not to say that I didn't really want to get in. But a man has to accept his limitations. Braces and youthful demeanor were my burdens. Couldn't really get around them.

22

WHEN I WAS fourteen, a book called *Thunder* was introduced to our school library. It was a fairly boring book with an exciting cover and writing on the back about how this book told the truth about sex, drinking, and drugs when others were afraid to. Two weeks later, following a parent-organized riot, the book was promptly removed. The principal said it had nothing to do with the ruckus made by the angry parents who didn't want their kids exposed to "that kind of garbage." And he claimed the book was definitely not being banned. The principal said, rather, that (a) the book was never meant to be in the school (that it was "ordered by mistake") and (b) that he had read the book and it wasn't very good anyway.

So guess what happened. Just about every kid in the school got hold of a copy, either by buying it downtown, borrowing it from a friend, or ordering it on the Internet. The lesson: nothing sells a book like racy scenes, and nothing lets people know that it has racy scenes like having it censored. Nothing.

So why am I saying this? Well, Arno was quite a party guy, and in the next few weeks, he not only supervised the sound, but he became something of a social coordinator. And with a few strings pulled, I actually got into a club or two. And because I am a young man in the prime of life (full of youthful vigor and extremely handsome), it might be imagined that I did some pretty crazy stuff. I was, after all, regularly impersonating Ace Frehley in front of hundreds of delirious women.

And since Arno began not only organizing post-show trips to clubs, but also began inviting fans backstage for parties in the more luxurious dressing rooms of Frog Bar and the Shoreline, there was a lot of activity. Believe it or not, even for members of a dopey imitation band like ours, life can get pretty wild. So here's the full truth. The sordid truth. The big disclosure. What you've been waiting for.

As for interactions with female fans, if I had any stories that might elevate my status as a man, then I'd tell them. I'd make the whole book about them. Every chapter would center around such a story. If it was a good story, I might even devote two chapters to it. I might even tell the story twice. Unfortunately, the story of my life as Ace Frehley is the story of romantic failure. This is not to say that I didn't turn a few heads. When you've got that guitar in your hand and you're muscling through a lead and your long (fake) hair is flowing across your shoulders, you are irresistible. And when you stomp backstage after blowing everyone away and the women see you all sweaty and tired like some kind of ancient Greek warrior fresh from the battlefield, you are nothing less than the most exquisite and exciting man that ever lived.

But take off your makeup, unroll the socks you've stuffed in your sleeves to make your arms look bigger, and remove the white tape to reveal your braces, and I assure you that you're no catch at all in the eyes of some KISS-loving vixen. I have watched desire come and go in countless women. They loved not me, but me pretending to be Ace Frehley. When the illusion was gone, so was the attraction.

Now, the able-minded reader might suggest that I keep my outfit on. If I was looking for love, a good idea might have been to continue playing the part of Ace. Strut around backstage for a while without taking off the costume. Indeed, I did this once when this extremely charming fan, aged, perhaps, eighteen, told me she really liked my moves out there. But while the makeup and the costume could stay on for a little kissing, the tape covering my braces could not. And, in this particular instance, after I sidled up next to this sweet baby and ripped off the tape to ask her what her name was (and maybe allow her to give the heroic musical warrior a small kiss), the only thing she could do was giggle and say, "Sorry, kiddo."

Now let me say that being the young guy did have some advantages with women. Backstage, as the band was hosting its little postshow parties, girls liked to talk to me, tease me, tickle me, poke me, and ask me silly questions about high school. But when the chips were down, I was more like a puppy dog than a man. I was little more than someone's kid brother hanging around a slumber party—not someone to be taken seriously.

But just as well, I always said. My heart belonged to Amanda, and I was better off not being tempted by those evil women. I am a gentleman and a man of honor. Better that the KISS FOREVER fans didn't take me seriously.

23   **OF COURSE**, romantic possibilities were not all that was available at backstage parties. That is, there was plenty of alcohol. And I am tempted to say that I partied like a freak, if only to agitate censors. I'm also tempted to say it because I've vaguely always wanted to be more of a rebel, not the clean-cut son of an orthodontist. But rebel I am not, and when the liquor and beer appeared, I just smiled at the gang, giving them a big glimpse of my braces to let them know that I couldn't really join in.

Now, I don't want to sound preachy. There were just all sorts of good reasons for my reserved behavior. Let me give you a big one: live with a delinquent older brother and you learn to stay out of trouble.

You see what it's like to be *in* trouble, and you learn to stay *out* of it. You realize that the price of such things is too high, and you decide you don't want to take chances.

My brother's problems didn't have much to do with alcohol. Actually, for some reason, that was something he managed mostly to avoid. I think that in my brother's universe of poor judgment, it was easy to stay away from alcohol because it was a clear signal of things that he might want to stay away from. Normally he just couldn't tell the difference between a good idea and a bad idea. He needed strong signals. Somehow liquor was a strong signal. But I guess I should point out that I don't entirely know all that my brother did. Maybe there's a whole side to this story that I don't know about. But given the fact that my brother got caught doing absolutely everything, it seems like the issue would have come up, if it was an issue.

And, let me also say, if on one or two occasions I did have a beer (or a gin and tonic, perhaps), I believe I would keep such stories to myself, because why would anyone write something down that would get them in trouble? I know, artistic freedom is important. And if such theoretical occurrences were relevant to my higher artistic aims, I might recount them. But occasional beers (and gin and tonics) seem largely irrelevant. Anyway, it's one thing to hold back on a story because you don't want to piss off censors. It's another thing to hold back because you don't want to be grounded by furious parents. Censors scare me not at all. Furious parents make my blood run cold.

24

WHATEVER. Other things happened that month as well that kind of end up being important. One of these things was homecoming dance, which was always in late October.

It was the tradition of Kensington High for students *not* to bring dates to this dance, so I was off the hook for trying to get Amanda to go with me. However, as many of the great failures of men often begin, I was feeling pretty cocky in those days, given my fame as a guitarist, and I decided that while I wouldn't ask Amanda to the dance, I'd ask her to get dinner with me beforehand. Why not? I was making some cash with the band. And doesn't every woman want to date a rock star? It was a bold move, but I was ready to take my chances.

I called her up about a week before the dance to make my proposal. I had spent a full twelve hours rehearsing my lines and preparing for any possible problem. I had emergency plans for her being busy, out of town, injured, sick with the mumps, etc. You name it, I'd thought of it.

I'd also come up with a few funny lines to warm her up to me. Cute things that I figured she'd laugh at. I'd make fun of the principal's hair weave, the poor state of the school parking lot, and the shocking affair between two teachers in the English Department. Once she was laughing and thinking how great I was, then I'd say something along the lines of, "Hey there, honey, what say we grab dinner before the dance? Sound like fun?" This, however, is how the conversation went:

AMANDA'S MOTHER: "Hello?"
ME: "Hello. Is Amanda there?"
AMANDA'S MOTHER: "Just a minute."

(PAUSE)

AMANDA: "Hello?"
ME: "Amanda?"
AMANDA: "Yes?"
ME: "This is Will. Will Brenner."
AMANDA: "Hi, Will."
ME: "What say you and I grab dinner?"
AMANDA: "Dinner?"
ME: "Yeah. Dinner."
AMANDA: "Now?"
ME: "No, not now. Before the dance."
AMANDA: "The dance?"
ME: "The homecoming dance. Are you going?"
AMANDA: "Oh. Yeah, I'm going."
ME: "Well, let's say we grab dinner."
AMANDA: "Before the dance?"

ME: "Yeah, before the dance. I'll pay. I'm in a
    rock band. I make money."

(LONG PAUSE)

AMANDA: "OK."
ME: "Great. Well, I'll talk to you later."
AMANDA: "OK."
ME: "Bye."
AMANDA: "Bye."

Needless to say, I still had a few kinks to work out
in my routine. In fact, looking at it now, it seems
that I really embarrassed myself. I knew that at the
time as well, I guess. But I was also kind of happy.
She did say yes. She didn't say, "Yes, and do you
happen to know that I love you, you beautiful
man?" But she said yes.

One of the problems with the call, however, is
that I neglected to set up a plan. Didn't pick a
place or say when I'd be by to pick her up. I
thought about this for about an hour and then
decided the best thing to do was call her back right
then. Best not to leave these things hanging for too
long.

This time I was a little smoother, but there
wasn't really much to say. I got her on the phone
again, said, "I'm a little embarrassed, but I forgot to
tell you when I'd pick you up. What say I pick you
up at six?"

"Six sounds good," she said. Then after a short pause, she said, "Will?"

"Yes," I replied.

"Did you know that I have a boyfriend?"

Another pause.

"Of course I know that you have a boyfriend," I said, although, obviously, I had no idea.

"You did? Oh good. He goes to a different high school. I wasn't sure if anyone knew."

"Of course I know. Of course. Everyone knows. It's common knowledge. So. See you at six? Next Friday?"

"OK."

"Bye." *Click.*

And that was it. In the matter of an hour I had gone from the exalted state of a man with a hot date, to the humble state of a man eating dinner with a taken woman. I can say without too much hesitation that it sucked. Sucked to be me, as they say. But I thought about it a little, and in order to delude myself into a state of some kind of emotional stability, I simply decided that Amanda's boyfriends had always been a problem and that this was no different and that surely I would be able to steal her away.

"Would that be right?" I thought. "To steal another man's woman?"

The answer to this question was no, but then I thought it over and decided that if you really thought about it, he had actually stolen Amanda from me. Think about it.

"I just need to be in the right situation," I told myself. "She just needs to spend time with me over dinner. That'll seal the deal. How could she like someone other than me? Just how could that be possible?"

I concluded that it wasn't possible.

25

THE WEEK passed slowly and painfully. The band practiced every day. On Thursday night we played at the Flame. I sucked. Or, rather, I was not playing my usual inspired guitar. After the Flame show, Mitch even said something to me.

"You, like, totally sucked out there, man," he said. "What's the problem? You've been sucking all week."

"Shut up, Mitch," Jim said. "He had an off night."

"It wasn't an off night. He sucked."

I opened my mouth to say something but then decided I really didn't want to argue with anyone. What really mattered anyway? The next day I would be going on a date with the girlfriend of some other guy. What else is there to say?

By the next day I was in heavy preparation for the evening's events. There wasn't really all that much for me to be doing. But I still felt obliged to prepare some lighthearted banter for dinner. We'd have to talk about something, after all. And I couldn't say what was on my mind. I couldn't say, "Dump that idiot and go out with me."

Fitz and Anthony, of course, were full of terrible advice.

"Bring her, like, two dozen roses," Fitz told me. "Women love that."

Anthony suggested that I show up for the date with two skateboards. One for me and one for her. "I have a friend in California who did that on a date and they totally fell in love."

"This is Chicago, Anthony," I said. "A man can't impress a woman with a skateboard."

The one thing that helped was the fact that my mother had decided to make me run all sorts of errands Friday afternoon after school, which sort of took my mind off my date. Driving my sister to ballet class was part of my list of duties. That didn't take my mind off Amanda, but it made me worry less.

"Do you think you'll kiss her tonight?" Olivia asked as I drove her to class.

"Put on your seat belt," I replied.

"It is on."

"It's not on. You're just holding it."

"Do you think you'll kiss her?"

"Put on your seat belt."

"Answer my question."

"Put on your seat belt."

"Answer my question and I'll put it on."

"OK. No."

Olivia put on her seat belt but tried to hold it away from her crumpling dress. "I think you should kiss her. That would be so romantic. You shouldn't be scared of some other boy."

"Thanks for the advice. I'll keep it in mind."

Funny. I found my obnoxious younger sister to be extremely funny and cute. When my older brother was obnoxious, I felt sick to my stomach and scared out of my mind. Makes sense though, I guess. It's not like Olivia ever knocked out anyone's teeth.

Anyway, by 5:00 I was back at the house staring at myself in the mirror and wondering why I didn't have bigger biceps. My hair was all wrong, and I suddenly decided that my eyes weren't symmetrical. One seemed to be lower than the other.

I put on jeans and a sweatshirt. Wanted to look cool and mellow. But I also sprayed on some after-shave I had gotten for Christmas the previous year. Seemed that might impress her.

By 5:45 I was in the car and driving to Amanda's house. At 5:50 I was parked a block away. Didn't want to be there too early. Didn't want to seem too eager. By 5:59 I was in front of her house. At 6:00 I rang the doorbell. Amanda's mother answered.

"Hi, is Amanda in?" I said.

"Yes she is," she said. "You must be Adam."

So that was his name.

"No," I said. "I'm Will."

"Will?"

"Yes. Will."

She paused. "I'm sorry," she said, and she looked like she really was. She was blushing. "Just a minute." She took a few steps back and then yelled up the staircase, "Amanda. Will is here."

In a few seconds, Amanda was bounding down the stairs.

"What's up, Will?" she said.

"Not much. What's up with you?"

"Not much."

We both looked at each other and smiled awkward smiles. I would have given all I had not to be there at that moment. But what could I do?

"What time will you be back, Amanda?" her mother asked.

"Dance ends at midnight," she said. "I'll be back between twelve-fifteen and twelve-thirty."

"All right. But not later than twelve-thirty."

"No prob," Amanda said, and then looked at me. "Ready?"

"Ready," I said.

I was not ready.

26 | I TOOK Amanda to a pretty nice Italian restaurant in downtown Kensington. I was careful to keep the loca-

tion of the dinner secret, just in case my brother decided to pay us a visit. Fortunately, he was nowhere to be seen when we arrived.

On the drive over, Amanda and I talked about various things. College, algebra, the Bulls, etc. And the small talk continued as we were seated at the restaurant. It was not riveting conversation. But riveting or not, it was at least not disastrous conversation, which is better than I had expected.

I will point out, however, that I was much more relaxed than I thought I'd be, and the conversation started to improve. Amanda gave me a long lecture about the evils of veal as we looked over our menus.

"They keep these baby cows in little tiny cages where they can't move," she said. "That way they can't develop properly and their meat becomes more tender. Isn't that cruel?"

I agreed that it was. I also rightly decided that I should not order the veal. Linguini. I decided linguini. With vegetables. Nothing cruel about that as far as I could tell.

By the time the food came, the conversation was actually going pretty well. I hate to admit to being such a boorish pig of a man, but the truth was that I actually didn't know Amanda all that well. So I was having a good time getting to know her, listening to her talk about herself.

She was also really nice, and as we were digging into our pasta, she started insisting that I tell her about my band.

95

"So I've been hearing a lot about KISS FOR-EVER," she said. "And I saw a poster for it the other day. It's pretty cool to play in a real band."

"It's not really a real band," I replied. I am a man of great modesty. "It's actually as fake as bands get."

"Yeah, yeah. I know you guys impersonate KISS. But that's still really cool."

"I have a great time."

"And you make money." Amanda flashed me a big grin.

"Yeah. Like I told you the other night. I make money."

Whatever, dinner passed with more light-hearted conversation. Amanda asked me more questions. I told her about a show that she could come and see—at a club that let in people under 18. And we talked about a million other unimportant things that suddenly seemed extremely interesting.

And it was really nice. I mean, really nice. So nice that I forgot that it wasn't really a date and that she had a boyfriend. But maybe I also decided that things were going so well that I might actually stand a chance with her—one day—if the boyfriend thing didn't work out. And as we walked to the car to drive to the dance, I was feeling a little more optimistic about the whole thing. Even if I never got to kiss her, it was pretty fun. And I know what you're thinking. You're thinking, "Yeah, right." But it's true. I'm not saying it was an ideal arrangement. But it was certainly less than the disaster I imagined it would be. And that counts for something. Counts for a lot.

So we made it to the dance at about 9:00. On the way over in the car, Amanda told me that her boyfriend and some of his friends were coming too. Harsh news. But I'm glad she told me. And I'm glad she was a little sheepish about it.

"Remember I said I had a boyfriend?" she said.

"Yes," I said, hoping that the next thing she said might be, "Well, I'm dumping his ass for you."

Instead, she said, "He'll be there later tonight with some of his friends from school, and, well, whatever." She paused. "I asked him before I knew I'd be having dinner with you."

Promising. But not the same thing as "I'm dumping his ass."

"No problem," I said, looking out the windshield as though I was concentrating on some difficult bit of driving and wasn't bothered. "No problem."

27 **ONCE WE WERE** at the dance, the official Will-Amanda part of the night was over. Too bad. But we had had fun. She went over to say hi to her friends. As far as I could tell, the boyfriend wasn't there yet. But I was keeping my eyes peeled.

I also found Anthony and Fitz pretty quickly.

"How's it going?" Fitz asked.

"Great. Her boyfriend's coming."

"What?" Anthony said.

"I told you guys she had a boyfriend."

"You didn't say he was coming to the dance," Anthony replied.

"Well, those are the breaks."

"You want us to help you kick his ass?" Fitz asked.

I gave him a look that indicated that our skinny bodies weren't going to kick anybody's ass that night. Then I said, "You know, we had a great time. Really. Not really in the mood to kick anyone's ass. I'm heartbroken. But I'm not mad. I knew. She told me. That was fair. But what am I going to do?"

Suddenly Anthony leaned over and gave me a hug.

"What the hell do you think you're doing!" I yelled, pushing him off me.

"I'm hugging you, man," he said. "You need a hug."

"Thanks," I said. "But I don't need a hug. Hug Fitz if you want to hug someone. You California freaks are getting on my nerves. This is Chicago. Don't forget that. We don't hug here."

So the dance was boring and stupid and dumb and at about 10:30 a pack of strange dudes from a strange high school showed up, clearly the boyfriend and gang. Amanda went and gave one of them a big hug, so that kind of blew my hopes that Amanda would send him packing that night.

I kind of circled around, keeping clear of everyone and counting the minutes till I could make a dignified exit. Finally, Amanda cornered me, boyfriend in tow, and said, "Will, this is Adam. Adam, this is Will."

"Nice to meet you," I said.

"You too," he replied.

Again, this wasn't what I pictured. And I felt vaguely entitled to throw a temper tantrum. Like, I wanted to beat this guy up and tell Amanda that she was a two-faced liar. But the fact was that she had lied about nothing, she had been completely nice to me, and it was only polite, after all, for her to introduce me to her boyfriend at some point. If she didn't, that might have been more weird. And to tell you the truth, this Adam guy seemed all right. Not the monster I was hoping for.

Anyway, after meeting Adam, I made the rounds, told Fitz and Anthony good-bye, and then headed home. Time for television, sweatpants, and ice cream. That was really all I had left in the world.

28 MONDAY afternoon, back to the KISS FOREVER grind. We had taken the weekend off. Monday afternoon was catch-up time. And we needed it. Like I said, I

had played pretty badly Thursday night. And the band was still kind of bothered about it.

"Are you going to suck today, kid?" Mitch asked when I showed up.

"Leave him alone," Phil snapped.

"No one sucked on Thursday," Jim added. "Anyway, Will's playing is so much better than yours that I'd knock it off if I were you."

"At least I'm reliable."

Mitch really had no case against me. But it was clear that my poor performance hadn't helped the band's morale. So I wanted to put in a good practice. And I did. I wasn't stellar. But everything was tight. Nothing to complain about.

After rehearsing about twelve songs, we talked about a few upcoming shows. Arno showed up for this part of the practice and told us that he had booked us at the Shoreline again, as well as at Frog Bar, and at another place called the London Underground, which was really one of the top places to play in Chicago. Basically, we were going to have a pretty full schedule through November and December.

My brother was scheduled to join up in about a week, if he didn't blow it, and his first show would be at a place called the Spark, which was the place that I had told Amanda about that let in people under 18.

"We can really get our name out there," Arno said. "It's a young crowd. But they pay just like everyone else. And they can really add to a band's rep. Plus it's a Saturday night. We should pack them in."

The Spark was in fact a pretty great place. I had seen a few concerts there over the years, and it was every bit as good as the Shoreline and Frog Bar.

"Can Jason be here Friday afternoon?" Arno asked me. "There are a few things I want to start going over with him."

"It's a day early," I said. "But it's close enough. If he stays out of detention I'm sure it won't be a problem."

"Well, if he can't make it, I can work with him on Saturday afternoon. No big deal."

I told Jason about the schedule when I got home that evening. He just shrugged and stared at me. Didn't look at all interested. In fact, during the previous three weeks of his probationary period, he had been acting like a complete jerk. Nothing specific. Nothing like the way he usually behaved. Just silent and sullen. Always kind of pissed off.

At dinner that night he was the same. He didn't say more than two words. And when the subject of band practice came up, he didn't join in. I don't know. Maybe he was nervous that he still might mess up.

Of course, you could also say that he was just learning to behave like a normal human being. There are all sorts of ways to be a jerk without committing crimes or beating someone up. In fact, silent and sullen is one of the ways most people deal with their anger, as opposed to destroying models of the Alamo or vandalizing grocery stores. Hard to imagine that Jason's foul mood was a sign of maturity, but the fact that he hadn't been thrown in detention for three weeks was a kind of miracle in our family.

All the same, I was starting to get nervous. If this was how Jason was going to be, I'd almost prefer him to be out starting trouble and getting nabbed by the cops.

And after dinner he was no different. He just stormed around all night. Worse, later on, when we passed each other in the upstairs hall, he bumped me so hard that I nearly fell over.

"What the hell?" I said.

"What?" he replied, staring at me with the kind of evil stare that only a guy like Jason can muster.

"You just pushed me."

"No, I didn't."

"Yes, you did."

"No, I didn't"

"Yes, you did." I kind of took a step toward him but then quickly backed off. I'm not that stupid. Suddenly my dad appeared at the top of the stairs.

"Problem, boys?"

Jason looked at me. "No problem," he said.

I paused for a second. I knew that if I said the right thing, I could make sure that Jason would never lift so much as a guitar stand for KISS FOREVER. And the truth is that part of me wanted to do this. But a bigger part of me didn't, and who wants to rat on somebody else to an adult? Anyway, all I said was, "No problem."

My dad looked at us for a second and then said, "Glad to hear it." He walked past us and into his bedroom.

Jason scowled at me again, and then headed down the stairs.

So pretty bad, in my opinion, Jason's pushing me around. But the next morning I discovered that he had done something much, much worse. Almost ridiculous really. But worse.

I have a pretty nice guitar. It's a Fender Stratocaster. Not the guitar Ace plays, but the only guitar I would play. I love the thing. And I saved up a long time to get it. My parents pitched in some money, but I shoveled snow around the neighborhood (there's a lot of snow in Chicago) and did whatever I could to scrape together the money—this was before I was bringing anything in from KISS FOREVER.

Anyway, that morning, I wanted to practice something that I thought of the night before. A lead that I was thinking about. I went to my guitar case and pulled out my guitar, set my amp very low because nothing pisses off parents in the morning like loud electric guitar, and started work. But as I began to play I noticed that there were some strange marks on the top of the guitar. Some scratches. Strange scratches that were definitely not there a day before. I unstrapped my guitar to get a closer look and suddenly realized that these were not any old random scratches but that they were, in fact, a word. And not just any word either. The scratches spelled out *J-A-S-O-N*. It wasn't large. They weren't huge scratches. It wasn't a huge word. But it was big enough.

No one was really out of bed yet, including my brother, but in another minute I was in his room, shaking him in his bed and waking him up.

"What the hell did you do to my guitar?" I yelled.

"What?" Jason replied, half sleeping.

"What the hell did you do to my guitar?"

"I didn't do anything to it." Still half sleeping. "I don't know what you're talking about."

"Your goddamned name is on it."

"What are you talking about?"

"You scratched your name in my guitar."

Jason sat up a little at this point. He was a little more awake, but he was silent for a few minutes. Finally he said, "How do you know I did it?"

"Because it says 'Jason.' Who else would do it?"

"I don't know," he said, and then there was a kind of smirk, which, let me tell you, made me want to punch him right in the face, although I never would have done this because it would have meant a certain and quick death. Finally he said, "Maybe Mom did it."

I paused. I didn't know what to say. What an ass. "Maybe she did," I finally said. "Why don't I go ask her about it right now?"

The smirk left Jason's face and he glared at me. He was silent for a moment and then he said, "Fine. Go ahead."

His glare was mean, and it didn't waver. He just kept giving it to me. But I have to tell you, and maybe I'm the biggest sucker in the world, his face kind of looked sad. Or disappointed. Sad and disappointed. Sad, disappointed, and mean. Kind of like the night he put me in the headlock in front of Amanda. Like he was actually surprised that I was so upset, like I was the one betraying him.

All I could think of was how angry I was and how completely insane Jason must have been to think that he could get away with it.

"I'll let you know what Mom says," I said, straightening up, and then stormed out of his room. I was serious. I really was. I had every reason to be furious. I had every reason to get his ass in trouble. But halfway down the hall, halfway to my parents' room, I kind of stopped. I thought I'd wait. I wasn't sure. Maybe I'd wait till Mom was awake. I went to my room and waited, but by the time my mom was awake, I hesitated again. I'll wait, I thought again, but by the afternoon, I had changed my mind.

Why did I change my mind? you may ask. Well, this is a question I actually asked myself. Not sure I have a good answer. I wasn't worried about retaliation. Jason would have been busted hard and I would have been protected. I guess that suddenly (and for the millionth time) I didn't have it in me to get him into trouble. Strange. I don't know why. I was furious. But it takes a lot to hurt someone else, and it would have been a nightmare for Jason if I had told on him. It's hard to throw that kind of nightmare onto someone else. Anyway, it didn't seem like it would do any good. I don't know. There are probably lengthy books on adolescent psychology that would say that not telling on Jason would only encourage his insane behavior. But let me say this, I've seen Jason punished hard (like sent to a juvenile detention camp, for instance), and it obviously never did any good. The fact is that in these situations, there's no good solution. There's only frustration. Like, frustration that the nicest thing you own, your prized possession, suddenly has your brother's name scratched into it. Whatever. Same problem I always had. This desire to throw him overboard—like he had finally crossed the line—and the simultaneous desire to hang out with him, have him like me, and to protect him even. All very puzzling. The thing was, I didn't know how long it would last. Like I've said, the impulse to cut Jason off was growing—like I had to do something before everything in my life was ruined by him. But it was just too confusing for me to come to any kind of real conclusion.

29 ANYWAY, aside from my familial struggle, life was kind of a bore for the rest of the week. Practices were pretty straightforward. School was slow. I felt pissed off because of the guitar, etc., etc., etc. Olivia was getting ready for *Swan Lake,* and she was attending nighttime dress rehearsals every single night that week, including late ones on Friday and Saturday nights. So the fact was that I wasn't even registering too strongly on anyone's radar.

I told Amanda on Wednesday about the KISS FOREVER show at the Spark, and she said she'd definitely be there. I didn't want to get my hopes up, but that made me feel a little happy. I was definitely glad she was coming. Then something else happened to change my mood, to make me feel pretty optimistic. I found out that Amanda had broken up with her boyfriend. I didn't get all the details. I just heard bits and pieces from Fitz, who had also heard only bits and pieces. But it was enough.

"It's definitely over," Fitz said as we were talking about it in the school cafeteria. "I have no doubt of that."

"You're sure."

"I'm sure. I heard it from three people, including Sarah Benning." Sarah Benning was a pretty close friend of Amanda's.

"Did you find out why?"

"I didn't find out, but I can guess."

"You can guess?"

"It's got to be because of you, man. It's too much of a coincidence."

"I don't know," I said, although I have to admit that this seemed like a good explanation.

"Well, it doesn't matter one way or another. The point is that she's free again. So now's your chance. And you'd better move quickly. You know someone else will ask Amanda out if you don't jump on it."

"Yeah. You're probably right. Well, I told her that there was a KISS FOREVER show she could get into. At the Spark. She said she'd come."

"She probably wanted to be available for you."

It was an appealing theory.

Anyway, my parents decided to let Jason come to practice that Friday. Like I said, he actually had another day in his month of probation, but since he had stayed out of trouble (as far as my parents knew), he was allowed to come along. Again, a month of no trouble from Jason was a miracle. Hadn't happened since he was four.

Jason showed up near the end of the practice, a little before Arno did. I introduced him to the band members, and everyone was pretty nice to him. Even Mitch threw in a "glad to meet you."

Arno arrived about five minutes later. He was carrying part of a set of amps he had rented for the show at the Spark. He set the equipment down and said, "This must be Jason."

"Yeah. This is Jason," I said.

"Ready to be a roadie?" Arno said.

"I guess so," Jason replied.

"Why don't you come out to the van and help me bring in the stuff. I can show you what you'll be doing. These guys probably have a few more songs to practice. Right, guys?"

"Right," Philip said.

We had actually just finished, but we decided to go over our opening again for Arno's sake. It was good having a manager. It was sort of like having a band mom. A mom might make you do things you don't really want to, but you know they're good for you in the end.

Jason and Arno carried in the rest of the equipment as we played, and they seemed to be getting along well. Arno was chatting away and Jason was smiling, which was pretty rare. It actually seemed pretty promising. And as Jason and I drove home that evening, he didn't even seem angry or sullen. This is not to say that he seemed particularly happy. But anytime Jason wasn't pushing me around or writing his name on something, things were good.

30 THE OTHER THING Jason got to do was drive the van, which he did the day of the Spark show with a kind of wild abandon that seemed to seep right from his deepest subconscious. I mean it. He was a maniac, and I really thought I was going to die. And I thought if I didn't die, Jason was definitely going to get beaten up by the band. All our lives were in danger, to say nothing of our precious instruments. But not so.

"Whoa, dude, where'd you learn how to drive?" they all yelled while laughing hysterically. They thought this was funny. Unbelievable. And Jason did too. Once everyone else started laughing, he started laughing too, and we ran about eighteen red lights and ten stop signs before getting to the club.

I will admit, however, despite my crippling fear, I did think it was just a little funny as well. I mean, I was well aware of the kind of toll this kind of behavior took on my life. But again, Jason had a strange kind of allure, and I almost felt a kind of pride in him as he was making everyone else laugh so hard. Shocking to say, really. But the other band members were all kind of rebels in their own way, and they seemed to be impressed by Jason's recklessness, so I couldn't help but feel this weird kind of pride.

All the same, as we finally arrived at the Spark (miraculously alive), I did start to wonder if all this was really such a good idea. The band members were seeing the funny side of Jason. But they didn't really realize that Jason kind of had a hard time shutting this side off. And I had seen the consequences of this side of Jason far too many times to trust it. But whatever. Nothing I could do at that point. Just had to hope for the best.

Anyway, we arrived at the club, and I do have to say that it was nice to have someone else carrying our stuff and setting everything up. Allowed me to focus on my makeup technique, which I had kind of been ignoring.

And I was also distracted for other reasons. I kept walking into and out of the dressing room, and peeking into the club. Couldn't help it. I wanted to know if Amanda had come. I wouldn't say I was nervous. But I was kind of antsy, to the point that the other band members noticed my strange behavior.

"Sit the hell down, man," Mitch said. "You're making me nauseous." And then, "You got a girl coming?"

When Mitch said this I must have turned bright red—right through my makeup—because everyone started saying, "Ooooooo, Will's got a girl coming," which (obviously) didn't make me feel calmer at all, especially because for all the times I went to scan the now rapidly growing audience, Amanda was never there. And by the time we finally went onstage, she was still nowhere to be seen.

The club, however, was completely packed. It's true that I couldn't help thinking that there was something wrong perpetuating the absurd and bizarre world of KISS. Perhaps it was best to let this foolish music disappear into memory, I thought. But once we had opened, I quickly changed my mind again. I say it so often that it's boring, but KISS music is so much fun to play, and as the crowd started singing along and dancing and screaming for Ace to "Jack it up, baby!" I bought into the whole thing, hook, line, and sinker.

I even almost forgot that Amanda had said she was coming, which is just as well, since she was nowhere to be seen. Finally, however, a few songs into the first set, just as Jim was spitting about a gallon of fake blood all over the stage, and just as I was getting to the ear-splitting crescendo of a solo, I looked out and saw Amanda staring up at me, right near the stage, smiling this huge smile like this was the greatest, funniest thing she had ever seen in her entire life.

So she had come. And she was close enough to smell the fake blood as it spattered around the stage. And she looked happy. Really happy. And I've got to say that it felt pretty great.

Anyway, the set ended, and Jim spewed more blood everywhere, and then Phil said, "We'll be right back." Everyone started yelling, "KISS,

KISS, KISS," so Jim gave everyone the finger, just to amp up the show a little bit, and in the next second, we were backstage, panting and laughing hysterically.

So normally, the break between sets was spent drinking gallons of water, fixing makeup, and trying to get some rest before we went back on. I did all these things, but quickly. I wanted to see Amanda. I quickly grabbed a big bottle of water, left the dressing room, and poked my head into the club. I spotted her after a few seconds, and (with some difficulty, given all the freak fans) I made my way over to her. She turned quickly when I put my hand on her shoulder, and then just started laughing. "You guys were so great," she yelled. "You were so, so great. I mean it. I can't believe how much fun that was."

Amanda was standing with a bunch of her friends, and they all laughed and said hi. It was pretty fun being the center of attention, and everyone told me they were having a blast and that they were coming to all my shows from now on. I told them they could come backstage after the show if they wanted (which seemed to excite them), and then I told them I had to head back to the dressing room.

"Got to get back into character," I said.

But before heading back to the stage door, I decided I had to check on one other thing. Jason. I was a little worried about how things were going, but when I got to the sound board, Jason and Arno were chatting and seemed to be having lots of fun. They had a big platter of french fries from the club's upstairs restaurant and were shoveling them into their mouths, and it was like Jason was some sort of well-adjusted, straight-A student out having a good time, getting along with everyone, not lighting anything on fire. Amazing. He even offered me some fries.

"Hungry?" he said, passing the platter over to me.

I took a handful, said, "Thanks," and then just kind of walked away. All very puzzling. Still, didn't have too long to think about it. People seemed to be ready for the show to start again, and I had to head backstage to get ready.

And the second set went as well as the first, as far as the music goes, and I have to say that having Amanda there and, apparently, impressing her, kind of gave me a boost. I belted out one lead after another with perfect precision. And I'm not being conceited. I can't even really take credit for it. It was just such a great venue, and Amanda seemed so into it, and the other guys were playing so well, that I just went with the flow. Really, I'm tempted to say it was one of the best shows I ever played.

Except for one hang-up.

It came in the middle of "Shock Me," the song that includes my three-minute lead. I went into it beautifully and, foolishly emboldened by having

Amanda in the crowd, I even threw a few extra little KISS-style power licks into the mix. I went up and down the fret board with dizzying speed, swinging my head back and forth in perfect (and fairly embarrassing) Ace Frehley style, completely losing myself in the song. But all of a sudden, in about the second minute of my lead, the volume on my guitar—and the rest of the instruments—shot way down. I looked up to see what Arno was doing but couldn't quite figure out what was going on. I kept playing, but I was now standing up straight, trying to get a sense of what was happening. And then, suddenly, all at once, it became very clear. Arno was pinned hard against the sound board, his face jammed up against a monitor. And there was Jason, holding his shirt collar and clutching his neck, shaking poor Arno like he was going to kill him. No joke. Jason had picked a fight right in the middle of my solo.

The show must go on, they say, but at that moment, the only thing I could think of was my own fury. I really couldn't believe it. I really couldn't. And everyone else was confused as well. Drums, vocals, and bass were now all you could really hear.

I unstrapped my guitar as I signaled to the other guys to hang on, and leaped into the crowd. Not that I had a plan. I certainly wasn't going to be able to hold Jason back. But I had to do something.

By the time I was making my way through the fans, Arno had already taken a few punches. The music had tapered off, but Jim soon began pounding out a bass line while giving an impromptu speech. He began screaming about how this was real rock and roll, and when real rock and roll was played, real-live mayhem occurred. "MAYHEM AND DISORDER. ROCK-AND-ROLL MAYHEM," he started shouting as he hammered on his bass.

As I finally got close to Jason and Arno, my problem of what exactly I was going to do was somewhat resolved. A bouncer showed up just about the time I did, and grabbed Jason. Now, Jason's a big guy, and not easy to restrain. But this bouncer was huge. Huge like a bouncer ought to be. And he immediately got Jason into a headlock—just as I was approaching.

"What the hell's going on?" I screamed, trying to make Jason hear me over Jim's improvisations.

"I'm going to kick his ass," Jason screamed.

"Your brother's nuts," Arno said. He was kind of shaking, but he still seemed calmer than Jason. All the same, he was pissed. "The guy is totally nuts," he said again.

At this point, from behind the gigantic arm of the bouncer, Jason managed to scream, "He's treating me like I'm some kind of idiot."

"I just didn't want you messing with the sound board," Arno replied.

"I wasn't messing with anything. I had an idea."

"Now's no time to be trying out ideas. We're in the middle of a show."

Jason again tried to struggle out of the bouncer's grip, but he wasn't going anywhere. At this point, the bouncer had seen enough to tell who was causing the trouble.

"I'm going to kick your ass," Jason yelled again.

"You're not kicking anyone's ass," the bouncer said, and started pulling him toward the door. It's funny, but even with a guy who was bigger than him, Jason could put up a fight. The bouncer was having a hard time moving him. But he was using some kind of mega death grip that only bouncers know about, and pretty soon another bouncer joined in. Eventually they pushed Jason through the exit and disappeared.

Mind-boggling. I was completely disoriented until Arno finally spoke up. "Your goddamned brother is totally crazy," he said again, and flashed me another furious look.

"I know, I know," I replied. "I'm sorry you had to see that." I took a deep breath and then looked around. Jim was motioning toward me with his hand as he kept chanting, "MAYHEM AND ROCK AND ROLL. ROCK-AND-ROLL MAYHEM."

I wasn't in the mood for any more rock-and-roll mayhem. But I didn't want to piss off a crowd of energized KISS fans. Maybe the phrase "the show must go on" is short for "the show must go on because if it doesn't, the fans and everyone you perform with will kill you."

"Go ahead," Arno said. "I'm fine."

So back I went. As I climbed onstage, Jim screamed, "HERE HE IS, TONIGHT'S ROCK-AND-ROLL WARRIOR." Then he took up the bass line to "Shock Me" again. In a few minutes, we were in the last verse and I was trying to keep myself together. It's easier to play guitar when you're inspired by a girl you like than when you're humiliated by your brother. But I made it through the song.

Still, the ordeal wasn't over.

As we moved into the next song, which would kind of move us closer to the end of the set, there was suddenly another commotion. I looked out into the crowd as there was all sorts of pushing and shoving.

And then, there before me, he appeared again. It was Jason. He had somehow managed to get back into the bar and was running through the crowd, dodging the bouncers and heading back toward Arno and the sound board. The strangest thing was that he kind of had a smile on his face, kind of like he was laughing, kind of like this was a game, like he was running from a linebacker or chasing some kid around with a stick.

And, to be perfectly frank, it *was* kind of funny.

Even Jim kind of saw the humor in it: "OH NO, HE'S BACK," he yelled into his microphone.

Time to take off the guitar again. But still, there wasn't much I could do, and I just kind of stood there dumbfounded at the edge of the stage. Jason made it as far as Arno and grabbed his shirt again, and was about to start punching, when the same first bouncer arrived. Amazingly, Jason now darted toward the stage, the bouncer clasping his back, and he might have made it all the way to the band, if the second bouncer hadn't shown up and grabbed hold of him. When this happened, there was a sudden jerking, and then they all fell to the floor, knocking over a bunch of the audience members, including, to my horror, Amanda. It kind of happened in slow motion—kind of the way something happens in a dream, when you can see something coming but can't stop it. Jim resumed his "MAYHEM AND ROCK AND ROLL" chant as I watched Amanda tumble to the ground, before a huge bouncer rolled over her. I stepped forward, wondering if I ought to dive off the stage and rescue her. But, thankfully, in the next moment, she was scrambling to her feet and, shockingly, laughing. And as Jason rolled over, also shockingly, he was laughing too. Laughing like this was the funniest thing in the world, like if he had the opportunity to be doing anything at this moment, this is what he'd be doing—wrestling with two humongous bouncers in a crowd of people.

But the fun was over. This time the bouncers had an even tighter hold on him—one had him around the waist while the other grabbed hold of his legs. And this time I was pretty sure they'd be watching the door to make sure he didn't make it back in. And I was right. I looked back at the band, watched Jim start pounding on his bass, and in the next second, we resumed the set—and made it through the next four songs without Jason wreaking any more havoc.

31

SO, A DISASTER. We were onstage for about fifteen minutes after the second fight, and I had been getting some pretty hostile looks from my bandmates. And once we were back in the dressing room, getting out of our gear, I really got an earful from everyone about Jason's behavior.

Mitch, of course, was the most pissed off. But I was used to that. More unnerving was how mad Jim and Philip were. They said a lot of stuff about being professionals and how we wouldn't be booked anywhere if we were known for starting fights.

"Especially between members of the band," Jim said.

After a lot of shouting and a lot of apologizing on my part, everything kind of died down.

"Let's just forget it," Jim finally said. "It wasn't your fault. But Jason definitely can't work with us anymore. I guess that's obvious. But he just can't. That was crazy."

Surprisingly, Arno was now the calmest. He just kept saying that he'd been through worse. But he also agreed that keeping Jason on was an impossibility.

"No objection from me," I said over and over.

Still, as important as all this was, there was also something else on my mind. After everyone had calmed down a bit more, I headed back into the club to find Amanda.

She was walking away from her friends when I saw her, which was good because I kind of wanted to talk to her alone.

"Crazy night," she said as I approached.

"Please tell me you're all right," I quickly replied.

"I'm fine," she said, smirking. "You have a crazy brother, but I'm fine." I was about to respond, but then she quickly added, "But you were great. I mean it. I had such a good time. Getting knocked over was nothing. Really. Kind of funny. But you were so great. That was so much fun."

I hardly knew what to say. Finally, I just said, "Thanks. It's a pretty fun job."

"Looks like it."

"So what are you doing now?" I asked, and then repeated my offer for her and her friends to come backstage.

"We'll all be hanging out," I said. "Even though members of my family aren't too popular back there right now."

Amanda smiled, but then said, "I can't. I kind of have to get home."

"OK," I said, and then paused. "But I'd like to see you again. Maybe we can go out to dinner again?"

"OK," she said, although, because I'm always afraid of disaster, I wasn't sure if she didn't hesitate a bit. But my tendency to overanalyze has gotten the best of me more than once. I decided not to dissect and evaluate the situation like I usually do. We were standing so close, and she had been so happy with the show, and she was giving me such a cute look, that it was hard not to feel a sudden rush of optimism. Complete, happy optimism. And so, unexplainably, and with the kind of bravado I never, ever exhibit (perhaps I was just taken with the moment of my glory as a rock and roller), I leaned forward, put my arm behind her back, and kissed her.

Now, kissing a woman is a difficult thing to pull off in most situations, but in the middle of a big club with people milling about, it's especially hard. There are people jostling you, people screaming, people trying to push their way by. Because of this, it's kind of hard to read the reaction of someone when you make such a bold move. And at first I thought that Amanda was kind of bumped away from me. Maybe it was what I was hoping for. It's what I hoped accounted for her strange move backward and away from me. But when I looked in her eyes, I knew that no one had bumped or jostled her. The reason we were not embracing in a torrent of love was because she didn't want to kiss me.

Rejection. No question.

"I'm really sorry," I said. "I just thought . . . I thought . . . What's wrong?"

She suddenly looked really upset and said, "Well, a few things, I guess. Or maybe just one thing." She paused. "I know that you probably found out that Adam and I broke up. And we did. But we talked on the phone last night, and I saw him this afternoon, and we decided to give it another shot."

"Oh," I said. It was a reasonable reason not to kiss me. Very reasonable. Highly reasonable. What a reasonable woman she was, not to two-time Adam. I really think that. I really do. She was doing the right thing. But I can also say that I wasn't happy. Nope. Not at all.

"Don't get me wrong," she continued. "I like you. I do. But I just can't get into anything with you right now. I know you understand. I know what you'd think if you were in Adam's position. But I feel really bad. I almost didn't come tonight. I really didn't want to lead you on. But I had a great time with you the other night. I really did. So I also didn't want to just blow you off, either. It's kind of a complicated thing to deal with. I really think you're great. But right now I really think we need to just be friends."

Of all the possible things there are to say in the English language, nothing wounds the heart of a man like the phrase "Just be friends." It will make you wake up at night sweating. It will make you sick to your stomach. It will make you want to tear your eyeballs out. I know. I'm an expert on this phrase. A total expert. "Yeah, I guess it is kind of complicated," I finally said.

What a nice guy I was.

She started to speak again, but I kind of let her off the hook. "Listen," I said. "This is no problem. I like you, but you haven't done anything wrong. I'm glad you came. I really am. I think you're great." Needless to say, I was masking my complete devastation. "And I guess the one good thing is that we are better friends. I don't feel so nervous around you anymore."

"Yeah," she said, laughing. "I used to think you were kind of out of your mind. I don't think you ever really said a full sentence to me."

"I don't think so either."

I smiled, then I told her good night and that I'd see her in school on Monday. The fact is that I was really kind of lonely. Kind of sad and lonely. No matter how good a sport I was, this was true. I felt kind of sad and kind of lonely. Things didn't exactly turn out the way I wanted them to. Still, in retrospect, I can safely say that events that night were only just beginning.

32

NEEDLESS TO SAY, I was not in a good mood as I returned to the dressing room. Disappointed, yes, but also completely ashamed. The girl the band had teased me about having in the crowd had just completely rejected me. And after what my brother had pulled, it seemed that I had entirely disgraced myself that night, and that my whole life was just a complete and total joke.

And this is kind of what I read in Jim's face as I walked into the dressing room. He had this look like he now seemed to pity me, like he wasn't even mad anymore. Or maybe it was a look of concern, like I had romantic failure written all over my face. And as I got closer, it seemed that this was definitely the look—one of concern, although it started to look much heavier than I would have expected. And then he stepped forward and said, "You've got to call your dad. On his cell. Apparently he's been calling. Something happened. With Jason."

I kind of didn't expect that. But I just walked right past Jim. Whatever it was, I didn't want to know. I'd had it with Jason, and I definitely wasn't in any mood to put up with him now. "Did he try to set the club on fire?" I asked as I pulled off my wig.

"No, but you've got to call your dad. On his cell."

"I'm going home now anyway," I replied. "I'll see him in ten minutes."

"No, you've got to call first," Jim said, now with much more gravity. "His cell phone. He said you had to call—not to go home. Again, an emergency."

"All right," I said. I rolled my eyes, but I have to admit that this didn't really sit well with me. Honestly, I started feeling a little freaked out. I stepped backward to the side wall of the dressing room where a phone hung, and as I picked up the receiver, I finally looked up at Jim and said, "Did he say what the emergency was?"

"I didn't take any of the messages," he replied. "The club manager did. But something happened. I think Jason took the band van when he got kicked out of here. And something happened."

It seemed like Jim knew more—but not enough to go any further, not the whole story. Still, if Jason took the van and Jim wasn't screaming, then it must have been something bad.

And now I started to feel a kind of sickening confusion. Like, I was still so depressed about what had happened with Amanda, and still so completely furious with Jason for being such a total idiot that night, but I was also starting to feel sick because I didn't want to know what my father had called about. But I had to call. Had to call my father.

It didn't take long to dial, but there was no answer.

"Are you sure I can't just go home?" I said to Jim.

Jim paused. "Look," he said finally, "I don't know what's going on. But you've got to call your dad. I don't know, but I think there's been some kind of accident."

Again, the way he said it—like he wasn't even freaked out about the van. I picked up the receiver and called again.

This time, my father answered, and all I could blurt out (before he said anything) was, "Is Jason OK?" And suddenly I realized that I was now much more panicked than I thought I was.

There was a pause. Then finally my father said, kind of haltingly, "Jason's fine. He's fine. He wasn't injured." Another pause. And then, still calmly, he continued, "But there's been an accident. With your band's van. Jason was driving. Apparently there was some kind of fight with you guys and he took it?" My father paused again, and I could tell that he didn't want to go any further. I wanted to yell at him to keep going, but I was dead silent because I didn't want to know what was next. I thought of Jason hitting some poor guy on the road, and what might have happened to him, and what an idiot Jason was, and how he had finally had it, had finally ruined everything for himself. I didn't want to hear it. I really didn't want my dad to say another word.

But he continued.

"Your brother was driving too fast," my dad said. "He came into the driveway too fast. He wasn't paying attention. And your mother was pulling out. To take Olivia to dance. One of the late dress rehearsals this weekend. They were in the car—just coming out of the driveway—when Jason came home."

I could tell my dad was struggling to steady his voice. I didn't want to know any more. But I finally said, "Is everyone all right?"

"Your mother's fine," my father said. "Banged up. A couple of broken bones. But fine. And Jason's fine. He's okay."

And then my father repeated this, again, trying to sound collected. "They're fine," he said again. "They're fine."

And then he paused. But it didn't matter. I knew what was next. The pause lasted. Then he said, "But Olivia's in trouble." And then he started to cry.

"Is she alive?" I said.

Pause.

"Yes," he finally replied, "she's alive."

"Is she going to be all right?"

And then there was another pause. The longest gap in time I've ever experienced. He said, "You've got to come down here. We're at Kensington Hospital. The emergency room."

"Is she going to be all right?" I asked again.

Again, a pause. A long one. "They don't know, Will," he finally said. "She wasn't wearing her seat belt. You've got to come here now. There's too much to explain." And then he hung up. And all I could feel was a strange kind of burning in my skin. Like everything was suddenly too bright. Like there was this very intense light beating down on me.

It's hard to say exactly what happened next. Who I told what to, where I threw my stuff, how I found my way out of the club. But I left. I had called a cab—the van was gone, after all. And in a few minutes I was being shuttled to the hospital.

I was more alert on the drive over. Or at least I remember it—remember some of it. I was in sweatpants, but my makeup was still on, and I remember I had a huge tub of cold cream tucked between my legs and I was trying to get my makeup off as we drove. And to be honest, I felt like a total idiot, like I was the biggest idiot in the world, dressing up like this. And I was thinking about Olivia and how she totally didn't deserve this. And I was thinking about my parents, and how much they must be suffering. And I was thinking about my brother. I wanted nothing more than to kick the crap out of him. But for some reason, the main thought I had about him was how much pain he must be in. I thought of this, and what an idiot he was, and how much he loved Olivia, and then I started to cry—right through the cold cream and the black-and-white mess that was now all over my face. Not what I would have ever expected. But it's what I was thinking. Pity. That's what I felt for Jason. I wanted to kick his ass. But I felt so bad for him. The idiot who thought only of himself. I felt so bad for him. I couldn't explain it. But it's what I felt.

33 THE EMERGENCY ROOM

wasn't too hard to find. Getting directions at the hospital is easy since almost anyone can see when someone's in trouble, that someone's been called there for a very bad reason.

And as impersonal and overwhelming as hospitals and emergency rooms can be, I've got to say this was different. The sleepy woman at the desk looked up suddenly when I said my name, and in the next second I was being ushered through a locked door, and then into a strange kind of back waiting room. It was not a very welcoming place— not the kind of place you ever want to end up. But there was more on my mind than my surroundings at that moment. As I stepped into the middle of this large, clean white room, I was suddenly face-to-face with my father.

He hugged me right away—kind of grabbed me from the side—but I have to admit that I wasn't interested in any kind of comfort at that moment. What you want at times like that is information. But there wasn't much of that to be had either.

"How's Olivia?" I quickly asked.

"She's going to go into surgery in a few minutes," my father said, again in a very strained voice—trying to be tough for me but unable to conceal his fear. And it was in this voice that he delivered more of the details, which were as bad as they could be. Damage to several major organs—kidneys, liver, and a lung. Severe head trauma that they were still evaluating—she was in a coma and her skull had been crushed in several places. And lots of broken bones. The list was longer, but it was hard to follow after I understood in such concrete terms what had happened. Likely brain damage, extensive internal damage, shattered bones. It was too hard to grasp.

I also did my best to piece together the story as well. I asked again how it had happened. My dad quickly said, "It wasn't Jason's fault," but the details didn't exactly match up to this. Jason had been speeding. Driving way too fast. He said he did eighty on the bigger street that led to ours. It was a thirty-mile-per-hour zone. Almost impossible to imagine how he was doing eighty. But he slowed down when he turned onto our street. Slower, but still driving like a bat out of hell. And when he came to our driveway he had no chance to react to my mother's car. He was fine. He had been wearing his seat belt. So had my mother. But Olivia hadn't been.

"But it wasn't his fault," my dad said again, with this kind of insane urgency. Half of me wanted to yell, "Then whose fault was it!" But I understood what my father was doing. There was an instinct to protect Jason, as guilty as he may have been, and for some unexplainable reason, I felt it too. For all the sudden and crushing sorrow I felt over Olivia, part of me was also deeply focused on Jason and the absolute agony he must be feeling. Again, don't get me wrong. There was anger. But in moments like this, I think human beings tend to feel love more than anything else. You're so desperate for some kind of redemption that a strange kind of love and forgiveness dominates everything else.

I thought about this all for a moment—what I had heard about Olivia, and what Jason must be feeling. And then I stepped back for a moment, kind of jarred by something I saw in the distance, out of the corner of my eye. I looked past my father and glanced through a doorway behind him. And there, in the hall, seated on a black chair, was Jason. He was bent forward, and his head was in his hands. He wasn't moving at first. But after another moment, he pulled his hands away from his face, then looked at the floor in front of him. And then he turned his head slightly, turned it in our direction. And then, suddenly, he was looking straight at me. It was a strange kind of look. It was a mix of anger and terror. I didn't know what to do. I was somehow paralyzed. In the next instant, he rose to his feet and then ran off down the hall.

34

I COULDN'T figure out whether to chase after him or not. But as I was standing there, thinking about him and about Olivia, the nurse arrived—or, at least, it was a nurse my dad seemed to recognize.

"Anything?" he said as she approached.

"Nothing new," she quickly replied. "She's in the best possible hands."

"Can I see her?" I asked.

"No," she replied blankly, pointing to a big door with a window in it. "She's in the ICU and about to go into surgery." She paused, and then said, "I've got to see another patient. But I'll be here if you need me." Then she walked away.

My father looked at me, then said, "Let's go see your mother."

I hesitated. Finally I said, "Hang on for a second," and then stepped toward the door to the ICU.

"Will . . . ," my father said.

But he wasn't grabbing hold of me. I guess he thought I had as much right to look as anyone.

It took some time to find her through the window—she was so immersed in tubes and shiny stainless-steel equipment. And I can't tell you how horrible it was when I finally saw her, finally saw a single hand and a small patch of skin that was the only part of her face that wasn't wrapped. A person attached to so many tubes and so many machines is such a strange sight—kind of a scene of ultrasophisticated technology in a state of useless failure. Like, the machines were all sparkling and high-tech, and there was a person dying beneath them. And worst of all, they prevented you from doing the thing you most wanted to do—grab hold of the person and tell her you love her. I looked for as long as I could, and then finally turned around to tell my father that I was ready to see Mom. But the words that came out were completely meaningless because I was crying harder than I'd ever cried, and could barely say anything at all.

35

MY MOTHER was in a small room in the emergency area getting a cast put on one of her wrists. The other was bandaged, and she had a huge neck brace and another cast wrapped around her shoulder. When she saw me, she suddenly lurched up. But the nurse quickly put her hand on her stomach.

"You've got to stay still," the nurse snapped.

My mom fell back on the bed, but kept her head turned toward me. All she could get out was, "Oh, Will," before bursting into tears for what looked like the hundredth time.

I stepped forward, but the nurse quickly turned and put her hand on me. "You, too," she said. "Plenty of time for that later. Right now we all have to be still."

My father had seen my mother already, but he didn't look any less shocked by all this. The whole thing was totally mystifying, and given what I had just seen through the window of the ICU door, it all looked very, very bleak.

"Does it hurt?" I finally asked.

My mother smiled through her tears and said she was fine. "And anyway, it's just a few bones. I'll be fine. I was lucky." And then she started crying harder for the same reason that I was now feeling sick to my stomach: the fact was that she *had* been lucky, but Olivia had gotten it so bad.

"I should have made her put on that seat belt before we even moved an inch," my mom finally said, and then started crying harder. Now my dad stepped forward and grabbed her hand (nurse or no nurse) and started telling her it wasn't her fault—something I guess he'd been saying a lot that night.

I wanted to grab my mother's hand too. I don't know if it's because I wanted to comfort her, or I wanted her to comfort me. It was hard to know what to do, and I was just about to edge my way around my father to take hold of her other hand, when I looked to my left, just slightly, and suddenly saw Jason standing in the doorway. I could now see him more clearly than I did in the waiting room, and I have to say that he looked like he had been through a hurricane. Totally dumbstruck, like he couldn't see or hear anything.

I didn't know how to react either. I just stared at him while he looked at my mother—I guessed for the first time. And then, in the next second, my mother looked up and spotted him and said, "Oh, Jason, I'm so sorry this happened. Come here."

But my brother just stood rooted in the doorway. Still shell-shocked. And then, once again, he walked off.

There was a pause. But in the next instant, my father had let go of my mother's hand. "Hang on," he said, and then ran out the door after him.

My father was gone for some time. I just sat there with my mother trying to piece everything together, and listening to her tell me how much she loved all of us. But my dad came back. In about ten minutes. And he said that Jason was in the waiting room. That he wasn't going anywhere. But that he wouldn't come back in.

I have to admit that it was kind of crushing. It really was. Still, my feelings were also shifting slightly. I thought about how horrible it all was. And I thought about how horrible it was for Jason. And then I thought about Olivia. And in the next minute I suddenly wanted to go out and break a chair over his head. I mean, what the hell did he expect? He always did whatever the hell he pleased. He never thought about anything but himself and his own good time. He had spent most of his life beating people up. And now he was surprised that something like this happened? It all seemed suddenly predictable—like, of course something like this would eventually happen.

"Will," my father said.

I was startled from my thoughts. "Yeah?" I replied, kind of dazed.

My father was looking right at me. "You've got to take it easy on him."

"I know," I said. "I know."

But the truth is that I didn't know what to think at all. Or what to say. Again, I felt terrible for him. I'm not saying I didn't. But at the same time, I wanted to kill him. Still, I managed to let the better side of me win. For the time being, at least.

36 STRANGE, but no one ever told us to "go home and get some sleep" that night. That's usually what you see on hospital TV shows. But not here—or, more accurately, not in our kind of situation. In fact, they needed us there. They even said as much to my dad. At midnight, they told him he needed to stay—"in case you have to make any decisions."

I'll tell you this, you don't want to make any decisions like that. It was a terrible thing to hear, the doctor saying that. And it was terrible to watch my dad have to look tough and thoughtful, like he could handle it. What a joke that anyone should ever be expected to handle something like this. He did tell me and Jason to go home. But only half-heartedly. I don't think he expected us to, and I don't think he really wanted us to leave him.

But it was a long night. A long, silent night. Just the three of us—my mother was asleep, sedated, in her hospital room. There wasn't much talking between us. And every time we tried to say something, it all seemed so foolish. Couldn't make small talk, because who cared about anything at that point? And there was the unspoken fact of Jason's role in all this. I mean, no matter how many times my father said "It wasn't his fault," no one there didn't understand that if he hadn't been driving like an idiot—in a van that he had stolen, no less—we wouldn't be there.

And Jason's obvious shock, and all of our sheer terror over the consequences of the accident, kind of kept us quiet, almost out of fear of what we'd say. Again, I think my dad wanted to protect Jason. I wanted to protect Jason. But it was almost like we most wanted to protect him from our own anger. My dad saying that it wasn't Jason's fault almost seemed like he was trying to convince himself, as though if this weren't true, he'd have his hands wrapped around Jason's neck, choking him to death.

Finally, at 6:30 in the morning, after a night of no sleep and tense pacing, a doctor came out to talk to us.

We all quickly stood up from the chairs we had taken on different sides of the room. The doctor looked at us, paused, and then started talking.

"We've stopped the bleeding," he said calmly. "One of her lungs is intact, but we had to remove the other. She lost part of her liver, but a good portion is still functioning. And she lost a kidney."

Pause. I think we all had questions. And we were all trying to process what we had just heard. But there was more, and we were all dead silent, waiting for the doctor to continue.

"Fortunately, the CAT scans from her brain look better than we thought they would. A lot of the swelling has gone down with the steroids we gave her, so we have a better sense of how it looks. Not as much damage as we were afraid of. But there is still damage. And to be honest, it's probably going to be a rough road ahead. There's a high likelihood of some kind of brain impairment. Maybe permanent. We won't know for a while. But there are therapies to deal with this kind of brain trauma. I'm not saying she can't recover. But we don't know yet. Still, the good news is that it does look like she's going to live."

I'm not sure what the doctor said next. What we said. How he left us. There was this strange kind of rapid calculation. Olivia was going to live. Relief. But it was relief shot through with shock. *Brain damage* is such a sickening phrase. It was hard to match these two feelings together.

And the confusion continued. My father drove Jason and me home. He insisted. No question, we were going home. He'd come back to be with my mother when she woke up. But we were going home.

And we did go home. Still in a total daze. And when my brother and I walked in, we were both totally silent. What could we say? It was almost as though we were afraid of saying anything because of what might come up—the accident, the incredible fear we shared. We both just went to our rooms. I can't say that I slept. I don't really remember. It was that strange kind of dizzy sleeplessness you feel when you've woken up too early and can't get back to sleep. You can't tell if you're dreaming or not. It was just all so frightening. And I have to admit that I was angry. But the anger was tempered with what I can only describe as a deep kind of sorrow. Sorrow for Olivia for reasons all too obvious. But also sorrow for Jason, because I couldn't begin to imagine having done what he did. I couldn't begin to imagine having been the driver of that van. It was too horrible to think about. Still, I couldn't get it off my mind.

37

IN THE NEXT few days, Olivia's condition didn't change. Jason and I were shuttled back and forth to the hospital, while my parents stayed there the whole time. We would have stayed nights too, but my parents refused. I think in their despair, they wanted to do something to keep things together, and trying to give some kind of order to my life and to Jason's seemed to be the best solution. And Jason and I didn't argue. My parents were suffering, and this was no time to pick a fight.

But the daze didn't leave. Jason still looked completely shocked—like he hadn't slept in days. And I still couldn't grasp the strange combination of anger and pity that I was feeling. For the next bunch of days, we kind of walked around in this strange sort of silence, speaking only when necessary, almost as though we were afraid of what we'd say once we really started talking.

Finally, after about a week in a coma, Olivia pulled out. But only barely. Only long enough to ask for some water. In very slurred speech. But a few hours later, she regained consciousness again, and the doctors started making assessments. It was still too early to say anything. But she was having enormous trouble moving her right limbs. And her speech was deeply slurred. And she had also lost sight in an eye.

No one knew if all this was permanent or not. They gave her more CAT scans. But they told us only what we had heard before—that it was too early to tell how extensive the damage was or how she was going to recover. That she had talked at all was good news, although she could only ask for water and didn't really understand where she was. But her motor skills—the slurred speech and the difficulty in moving—were not good signs at all. Still, again, it was too early.

It was that night, the night of the day that my sister first asked for water, that the strange, thick silence between Jason and me finally broke, although in a sort of sidelong way.

We were back at home. My parents were at the hospital. It was the same routine. My mother and father wouldn't leave Olivia, but they insisted Jason and I go home each evening. We had been home for about an hour, and I was sitting at my desk, looking over a stack of homework my teachers had sent—nothing too hard, but enough to keep me from falling too far behind. Jason knocked, asked if he could come in, and soon he was sitting on my bed, across from me.

To describe what had passed between Jason and me that week as silence isn't completely accurate. We had, of course, spoken to each other. But mostly about nothing at all. Things like, "Dad's here." Or, "I've made something to eat, if you're hungry." And we even spoke briefly about Olivia—but mostly vague and quick expressions of grief, followed by hours of saying nothing. But we hadn't really spoken, not about the accident. I could tell, however, as Jason looked at me from my bed, that this was going to be different. Still, it wasn't entirely what I expected.

"I just wanted to apologize for picking that fight with Arno," Jason said softly. "It was really stupid, and totally my fault, and I have no idea why I did it."

It was kind of a surprising apology, and part of me wanted to say, "That's what you came in here to say?"

But in a strange way, Jason was trying to connect with me, or he was trying to get to something. I don't know, people never really quite say what they mean, and from the look on Jason's face, I could tell that for whatever he said, his feelings were pretty intense.

"And I'm sorry I took the van," he continued. "I know I always say stuff like this, but it's not going to happen again. I'm not going to do anything like that again. I'm never going to do anything wrong again."

"I know, Jason," I said. "I know."

"But you have to believe me, Will." He was now pleading with me. "It's going to be different. I'm not going to cause any more trouble. I'm really going to be different. I mean it. I don't even know why I picked that fight. I really like Arno. I liked that job. I was grateful you got it for me. I'm really sorry."

Jason looked up at me desperately, like he was going to continue, but at this point he looked more like he was fighting back tears than thinking of what to say next. No tears fell. Just glassy eyes, a tense stare into the space ahead of him, and silence. Still, I could tell he was in pain.

I sat next to him on the bed for some time while he stared, glassy eyed, across the room. But the talk was over. I don't think he could have said anything if he had wanted to, for fear of the tears. But the stare finally ended and he finally stood up, ran his hands across his face, and then walked out of the room without saying anything else.

It was a hard thing to figure, but it was pretty obvious what Jason was thinking about. It wasn't beating up Arno. But despite a certain kind of clarity at that moment, it also left me with another, different, strange kind of feeling. It was like I suddenly didn't know Jason at all. Or I didn't know him now—I didn't know this guy who had just been in my room. And then, for some reason, I thought of something that he had done several years earlier, on my thirteenth birthday.

Jason had been mowing lawns all spring and early summer for a guy who liked to hire young trouble-making types. It was a good deal for Jason—his boss knew just how to handle him, and Jason made some money. Anyway, when my birthday rolled around and we had our customary family party, Jason presented me with this huge, heavy wrapped box. I didn't really want to open it, given Jason's usual behavior toward me at times like this, but I finally did and discovered that Jason had bought me a new guitar amp worth about five hundred bucks. It was a top-of-the-line amp—something I never could have gotten on my own—and it was, in fact, the amp I would eventually use in all my KISS FOREVER shows. So, high end and professional grade.

I didn't know what to say. Frankly, I thought he had stolen it. But Jason said he had saved the money, and my father even said he had been there when he picked it out.

Finally I just said, "I can't believe this."

Jason just stood there smiling. And I could tell how happy he was. Olivia started playing around with it, and my parents shook their heads in a sort of confused disbelief, and I just sat there thinking that this was now the nicest thing I owned.

But a few minutes later, Jason kind of snapped out of it, and said, just to make sure that no one thought he was going soft, "So that's it for you, Will. The last nice thing I'm doing for you for a while. So don't get used to this kind of treatment."

He kind of had a scowl on his face, and I could tell he was being tough, but this was a ton of money for him, and it really was thoughtful just because this amp was so obviously something I'd love. The point is that I was sure that for whatever hard-guy act Jason was now trying to pull, he felt good that I was so happy.

Again, I'm not exactly sure why I thought of all this, other than maybe I was thinking how Jason had such a strange, mixed personality. I thought about how happy Olivia could make him, and how happy he had been with Arno, eating french fries and chatting at the back of the club, and how happy he seemed when he bought me that amp. But mostly, at this point, I was really wondering how I felt about him. I wondered how I felt about Jason, and what he had done, and what our relationship was all about. And I couldn't help wondering just what was going to happen between him and me. I hate to say this, but I kind of thought that I was just fooling myself. Like Jason could buy me guitar amps and sit on my bed and fight back tears, but that some kind of barrier between us that had been started long ago was now nearing completion. Still, I'm not lying when I say I felt extraordinary pity for Jason that night that he sat on my bed and said he was sorry for picking the fight with Arno. Strange that you can have feelings like that despite all the reasons that you should feel otherwise. I really did feel a deep kind of compassion for him. Almost indescribable.

Still, I couldn't help but feel like it was never going to get better, and like he and I were finally at some kind of breaking point.

And, in fact, that turned out to be true.

38 IT CAME about two weeks later— now three weeks after the accident— on a Saturday night. Things were the same with my sister. Or, I should say, they were better, at least in specific ways: she was talking more, she could move her body, etc. But she still slurred her speech, her right side moved very slowly and with a lot of difficulty, she'd still lapse into periods of confusion, and she still couldn't see out of her right eye. Whether or not it was all permanent, no one knew. That she was better was something, but no one wanted to hope for too much, given all that was wrong with her. The dam-

age to her lungs alone would change the way she lived for the rest of her life.

But my parents had started sleeping at home again. They stayed at the hospital till Olivia fell asleep, and then they'd come back. They had only just started doing this, just as Jason and I had only just started resuming something of a normal schedule ourselves. We went back to school, did our homework as best as we could, and I even made my first appearance at a KISS FOREVER practice, although the band was definitely on a break. "Take as long as you need," Jim told me. "We're not going anywhere."

But, of course, normal routines do not make a normal life, and as we all went about our business, we all knew that our lives had become very, very different.

And there were times where it was specifically hard, specifically terrible. Like that Saturday night. My parents were home from the hospital—Olivia had fallen asleep for the night—and my mother started having trouble breathing. It was because of the injuries to her ribs and her collarbone. The doctors told her it might happen. It was no reason to be alarmed. But they said if it did happen, she should go to the hospital right away.

I was at home trying to help out, but my brother was at the YMCA, playing basketball with some other guys, after my parents encouraged him to go.

So it was my dad and me trying to help my mother as best we could.

"We've got to take you in," my father said several times.

"I know," my mother said weakly. "I just feel so stupid." She was crying by this point, and while the pain might have been part of it, more of it was Olivia. My mother said as much. She kept saying "I'm fine" through her tears, followed by "I can't believe what's happened to my daughter."

Pretty rough. And a normal thing to hear in those first weeks after Olivia's accident, as shocking as it always was. I can't quite describe what it's like to see your mother in such a state of sadness, but it's not that hard to imagine. Just think of a person you love very deeply in excruciating and constant psychological pain. That's what it was like that night.

At any rate, my dad was helping my mother on with her jacket when the telephone rang. Just about everybody in the neighborhood was on permanent duty helping us out, and we had gotten about ten offers that day alone. But when my father picked up the phone, I could tell this was about something else. It was for my father, and I'd heard the conversation before.

It was the police. Jason had been arrested.

"For what?" my father said into the phone, and then he abruptly ran his hand across his forehead and through his hair. But his reaction wasn't one of anger. It was weariness. And as he continued to say things like, "I see" and "I understand" into the phone, his expression continued to show fatigue more than fury.

"And what will bail be?" my father said. And then, after a pause, he said, "OK. OK."

But then they started talking about other things. I could tell the cops were worried about my father—were sorry for him. Kensington was a small enough town and obviously the cops knew my parents pretty well. And they had been at the scene of the accident. I could tell they were asking about Olivia.

"She's doing as well as can be expected," my father said. "But it's bad. There's no way around that."

There was a pause.

"Yeah, her right side. Yeah. One of her eyes."

Then there was another pause, and my father finally said, "Can I ask you for a favor, Tony? Can I send Will down to pick up Jason? My wife's doing really badly right now—with her breathing—and I have to get her to the hospital."

There was a pause.

"I know there are problems," my father finally said, "but it would really mean a lot to me. It would really help me out."

Another pause. This time longer. Then, "I understand. I understand. Thanks, Tony. I appreciate your doing this for me. I'll send Will down with my credit card."

As my father said this, he wiped his hand across his cheek, said "Thanks again," and then hung up the phone.

He looked up at my mother and me and then just shook his head and groaned, "Well, he's been arrested. Shoplifting DVDs from the mall. He had about a hundred bucks worth stuffed down his pants. And apparently he and his basketball buddies broke off a stall door in the bathroom. Do you mind, Will? Do you mind picking him up?"

My mother's breathing was now even worse, but she wasn't crying anymore. She just looked like she was in agony. It was a strange look, though, because she didn't even seem pissed.

"Maybe you should just leave him there for the night," I finally said in a hostile tone. It seemed like a good idea to me. Probably what Jason needed. Probably what my parents should have been doing all along.

My father was silent for a second, then said, "No. We've got to go get him."

My mother said the same. Through her slow breaths, she said, "We need to get him home."

And as they said this, as they said they wanted him home, I was now feeling a kind of blistering and overwhelming anger, an anger that I hadn't ever felt before. I just couldn't believe what Jason had done. That night with the DVDs. The night of Olivia's accident. And for his whole goddamned life. And all I wanted to do was hurt him—hurt him as bad as I could.

Finally my father stood up and said, "Let me get you my credit card." Then he walked off to his study.

I looked over at my mother and almost started screaming—almost started yelling that Jason should stay in jail for the rest of his damn life and that she and my dad were crazy if they didn't kick him out of the house that night. But my mother was again struggling to get her coat on, and all I could do was walk over and help her out.

39 AND AS I walked out of the house and down the side path and out to the car, my anger only grew. I thought about Jason beating up Arno that night, and laughing about it at the time, and then stealing the van and ramming it right into the back of my mother's car, and how it never occurred to him how anything he did might hurt other people. And I thought about what he had done that night. Stealing the DVDs and vandalizing the bathroom, and I just couldn't believe that he did it again, now, in the midst of the worst thing my family had ever faced—something he had caused. And I thought of the weary look on my parents' faces and how they didn't need this at all. And as these things passed

through my mind, all I could think was that this was it. This was it for him and me.

And as I turned the ignition and pulled onto the street, the thoughts just continued. The whole thing was typical, and as I thought about the conversation we had just had in my room, and all his assertions that he had changed, I could barely contain my rage. And why DVDs? It just defied reason. I even thought that I might feel better if he had drunk a lot of whiskey and started a fight. There might have been something a bit more acceptable about that—it might have reflected the situation a bit more. I could have told myself that he was probably feeling as rotten as I was and then got into a fight. But DVDs? There was also something so irreverent about it. Every time I strummed a chord or figured out a math problem in those few weeks after Olivia's accident, I was gripped with a desperate kind of fear, and thought about how pointless everything was. Pointless like, your sister is lying in the hospital and might never recover and why bother doing anything? But at least there was a counterargument. At least you could say something like, "It's important to get good grades, get a good education, a good job, raise your own family, blah, blah, blah." But there was no possible reason you could come up with for boosting a hundred dollars worth of DVDs. And because of that, it really just seemed like such an affront to Olivia. Like, you'd think he might have been through enough to have suddenly realized that stealing crap with his stupid friends was ridiculous, and said, "I've got to take off, guys. I've got better things to do."

And there was also a more personal side to my anger. As I drove through Kensington on my way to the police station, another issue unfolded in my mind. There were plenty of times I resented Jason, just like everyone did in my family. But I never really gave up. No one gave up. And no one gave up because there was always this hope that he'd somehow come around. It was like my father said: "Some people just need more time; you need to be more patient with some people." But now, as far as I was concerned, Jason had blown it. All the apologies, all the sorrow, all of it was a lie. And as I thought of my mother crying in our living room, blaming herself for Olivia, I could no longer think of a single reason to show Jason a bit of compassion.

And all the times I had to suffer through his tantrums and bullying resurfaced as well. There were plenty of times that I wanted to retaliate, that I wanted my parents to retaliate, and to retaliate hard—like military school, or letting him spend a night in jail before bailing him out. But somehow, Jason was always let off the hook. And I was just as guilty. I always let Jason off the hook. I knew that this night was the night that I'd be delivering some kind of final statement. I was going to let him know that as far as I was concerned, he and I were finished, and that if he pushed me around or stepped out of line, I'd be the first one to put a stop to it. Maybe he'd win in a fight, but I'd be ratting him out to Dad or even the police if I saw him doing anything wrong. It wasn't a threat. It wasn't meant to get him to shape up. It was a way of telling him that he'd already failed and that he'd blown all his second chances and that as far as I was concerned, it was too late for anything. He'd caused me nothing but trouble his whole life, and from my perspective, he really was no brother of mine at all.

By the time I was parking outside the police station, I was almost shaking in my anger. Admittedly, I did feel a little bit foolish, a little bit self-righteous, the younger brother with the braces there to bail out his older brother. But the anger was real. I couldn't talk myself out of it. And I was in the right. There was no question about that.

When I walked into the police station, still kind of shaking, I immediately went up to the front desk. The entry hall was bright, and there were cops walking around holding clipboards and entering and exiting doors. I told the cop at the desk who I was, and in about five minutes, Officer Hendricks—Tony—appeared.

"Hi, Will," he said.

"Hi, Mr. Hendricks," I replied.

"Your brother will be here in a second," he said.

Then Officer Hendricks leaned over to the cop at the desk and said, "This is Will Brenner. He'll be taking Jason Brenner home tonight. His dad sent along his credit card. Mr. Brenner will come in tomorrow to sign everything else."

As I got out my dad's credit card and handed it to the cop at the desk, my brother suddenly came through another door at the side of the room. I looked up, and he looked back at me, flashing the glare that I had come to know so well. It was angry, threatening, and challenging, like he was daring me to yell at him. It was a dare I was willing to accept that night, and as the cop ran the credit card through the machine, I started going over what I was going to say to my brother, how I was going to go after him.

Jason moved behind me, out of my gaze, as the credit card machine printed the receipt. In the next instant I was signing my name, and then I turned to see my brother zipping up his jacket. I looked at him, and he looked right back at me. I was steeling myself for the fight. But I also couldn't help but wonder how far it would go. And for the first time that evening, I felt slightly unsure of myself. I wasn't chickening out. I just wondered where it would go.

"I don't want to see you down here again, Jason," Officer Hendricks called from behind the desk. I looked up at him. Useless parting words, but he was a friendly guy, and he relaxed me for a moment. But just as quickly, I tensed up again. I wasn't letting my guard down. No way. I knew that once we were out those doors, a lot of baggage was going to be unloaded, and I wasn't going to let Jason get the best of me this time.

Jason was actually ahead of me by the time I made it to the door. By about ten feet. He was outside first, and I was taking quick steps to catch up with him. In another minute, I was at his side, once again calculating how to begin the speech that I felt I had been waiting years to give.

But as I looked over at Jason and he looked back at me, a strange kind of feeling overtook me, and for the first time in a long while, maybe for the first time in all the years that seemed to have been leading to this, I felt like this glare I was getting from Jason had softened slightly. I wasn't sure if this was new, or something that I was seeing for the first time. It was definitely the glare that Jason always gave me. His shoulders were square, his head high, but there was something else, a strange kind of regret in his eyes. Real regret. Not empty apologies delivered with a glassy stare. And I've got to tell you that it almost broke my heart.

I did everything I could to resist feeling sympathy for him. I really did. I wanted only to retain the hostility that had possessed me on the drive down. I thought about how unfair Olivia's accident was, and how miserable I felt about it, and how Jason had done nothing but aggravate the family's pain. I thought of my parents and their sadness, and of my mother at home crying and blaming herself for Olivia, and how Jason had been out stealing things at the mall. But as we got into the car, and as I turned on the ignition, still thinking hard of where to begin, still thinking of a first line to start my speech to tell him that I was through and that he was out of second chances, I could only manage to ask him if he was all right.

"Are you OK?" I asked.

"I'm fine," he replied, trying to affect a sort of toughness. But as I glanced sideways, pulling from the parking lot onto the street, I noticed that he was starting to cry. And as I began to wind my way back through Kensington's quiet streets, my anger started slipping away. I tried to get it back. I really did. I really tried. But it was slipping away. I felt like a sucker, wondering if I was once again being duped by Jason, but I have to say that there was nothing I could do.

I looked over at him again and he looked back at me, his tears now coming full force, in uncontrollable sobs. Still, he managed to say something through the tears. "Will," he finally said.

"Yeah?"

"I didn't mean to do it."

"It's OK, Jason."

"I just did it. But I didn't mean to."

"It's OK."

"The things I said in your room, I meant them. I don't know why I did it."

"I know. It's OK, Jason."

"But you have to believe me. I wasn't lying when you and I were talking in your room. I don't ever know why I do anything."

"It's all right, Jason," I said.

"But I'm really sorry. I'm really sorry. For everything."

"I know, Jason. I mean it." And I did. As strange as it was, at that moment, I really did mean it.

It was very strange. There are probably those who'd say that Jason's tears were a joke, that he had lied too much already, that he shouldn't get off so easy. Maybe. Some people might also point out that telling me he didn't mean to do it was a ridiculous explanation. Jason was responsible for his own actions, right? Maybe. Maybe that's the truth. And I'm certainly not here to let anyone off the hook. But I'll tell you one thing, one unavoidable fact: my anger was gone. Totally gone. And it wasn't coming back. There was nothing I could do. I wasn't going to deliver any kind of final speech about how he and I were no longer brothers, and I realized at that moment that I never would, no matter what he did. That was simply something that I would never, ever say to him.

As we continued the drive back to the house, I kept thinking about something my dad once said to me. Jason and I had been having a hard time one day, and that night my dad told me that one day things would be easier with Jason, that things would be easier between us, that Jason and I would have a normal relationship. The truth is that I didn't need to hear that—it was something I had been counting on and looking forward to my entire life. It was the one thing that always kept me going, that made me feel like there was a point to putting up with him. But now it seemed that might not ever be true—that it might not ever get any easier.

But mostly, I kept coming back to an image that I think had been in the back of my mind for most of my life. I used to imagine that one day we'd be adults with families of our own, meeting for some kind of barbeque or holiday dinner, he and I with some kind of job or other, with houses somewhere in the suburbs of Chicago, with lives of our own, both squared away, stable, happy, untroubled. We'd talk about our lives, our parents, what we wanted to do, what we wanted our kids to do, and maybe wonder why things had always been so difficult for us, maybe even talk about why Jason had had so much trouble making his way through adolescence. This was always the image that made my relationship with Jason a little easier. It was what got me through the rough patches.

But for the first time, this idea started to seem like it really might be just a fantasy, that it might be a fiction, an impossibility. There are always ways for people to change, to grow, to make a new start. But for the first time in my life, it occurred to me that this might not happen. I thought that Jason might never quite get it together, that he might never really be out of trouble, that he might have a hard time holding a job, making a living, and that this might continue well into his life, maybe until the day he died. Nothing seemed inevitable or likely about him changing. It wasn't impossible. I just didn't know. Had no idea. But the point is that I also didn't care. It wasn't that I was giving up on him. It's just that for the first time, I wasn't really pinning our relationship on any kind of imaginary future. The future would be what it would be, and at that moment I didn't care how it turned out, at least in terms of how I felt about Jason. The main feeling I had, the main thing I kept telling myself over and over as I stared at the road ahead of me, was that I'd pick Jason up from any police station that ever arrested him, that I'd always come up with the money to bail him out, and that if he ever did something really bad, like something that was so bad that it sent him to prison for a long time, I'd write him and visit him and take care of his things while he was away. I'd always be there for him. I'd always bail him out. Even if he destroyed my guitar and beat up my sound guy. Even if he went back on his apologies a million times. It didn't matter. It really didn't. I'd always bail him out. No matter what. Funny. It was like I had been waiting for years for this guy to change, but the only one who seemed to change was me.

Again, don't get me wrong. I never was and never will be a defender of the things Jason's done. But as we finally pulled into the driveway, as I continued to think about what had happened to Olivia, and how desperately sad I felt, how desperately I wanted her to get better, I knew that the very last thing that I would ever be capable of doing would be to tell Jason that he had no place in my life anymore, that he was being cut off, that he wasn't my brother, that I wouldn't pick him up from the police station.

Funny how you can feel that way about someone who picks fights with you and steals DVDs and terrorizes your friends. It was very confusing. But also undoubtable. As feelings and opinions go, this one was a true one. I still have trouble explaining it.

40

MY FATHER came home later that night—my mother stayed over in the hospital—but there wasn't a lot of yelling when he came back. He went into my brother's room, and they had some kind of talk—I was sure of that—but what was said, I have no idea. I think my father probably said and did the same kinds of things I did, and for the first time I think I understood how my parents viewed the whole thing—you ground a kid, take him to therapy, pay for tutors, even let doctors pump him full of medicine, but cutting him out of your life just isn't an option. In fact, the more he messes up, the more you hold on. I don't know. Maybe not. Like I said, I don't know what my father and Jason talked about that night. But there was no yelling. And Jason wasn't kicked out of the house. And if there was ever a night when this was going to happen, this was it.

Two months later, Jason was put on trial for the DVD thefts. It was the same as always: stern lectures and my brother apologizing. But the sentence wasn't as bad as it could have been. The judge put him on a special kind of probation that made him show up to a detention center every day after school. He basically let him off easy, telling him that what happened to our sister "probably clouded his judgment." Seemed like crazy logic to me, frankly. Who knows, maybe the judge felt like I did—wasn't willing to send Jason up the river. It's possible. But I was happy Jason got off lightly. I was ready to cut Jason all sorts of breaks, whether he deserved them or not.

But the truth is that I wasn't really thinking too much about Jason's trial at that time. No one was. Not even Jason. Olivia had been walking for two weeks and her speech was a little less halting. It was a long way from pirouettes—they would never come again, the doctors told us—but no ballet move could ever have made anyone as happy as we were with those first few jerking movements across the floor. Seriously. You can't imagine how happy you can be watching someone walk. She still had a long way to go. But it was incredible to see that.

Since I'm winding things up, I should also add that by the time of Jason's DVD trial, KISS FOREVER was kind of back on its feet, which was good since I was ready to get back to my normal life—if you can call putting on makeup and spitting blood in front of hundreds of people normal. And there was Amanda, whom I recklessly decided might actually like me after all. I was a glutton for punishment, and continued to scheme and plot over her. But I was also pretty sure that nothing would ever happen. Still, what was I supposed to do? You don't get to choose who you have a crush on. And things with my brother went back to normal. Lots of angry stares, although not quite so many dead arms. I was relieved. I didn't think I could take a new kind of situation where we were suddenly being all emotional with each other. Not my style. I even tried to get him his job back with KISS FOREVER. But this was out of the question. "No goddamned way," the band members all said. But I think they were glad enough to see that I made the proposal, given all that Jason and I had been through.

And we had been through a lot. And given the fact that Jason had somehow grown another inch during all this, there'd probably be at least a few more years of dead arms and angry stares. But maybe I'd grow too. And start lifting weights. And become as strong as him. It was possible. Unlikely, but still something I was willing to hope for. Like a lot of things.

also by Michael Simmons

pool boy

It's like this. I used to be one of those kids who could coast through life without having to do any of the unpleasant things most people have to do. I'm fairly smart, pretty athletic, and some have even told me I'm reasonably handsome. The key to the cushy life I used to lead was that I also used to be rich. Not fairly, or pretty, or reasonably, but extremely. Extremely rich. All that changed one day when cops and guys in suits showed up at my house and told my dad that he was in big trouble and that he owed the U.S. government ten million dollars.

Dad tried to run. He pushed one of the cops and tried to make a getaway out the back. It's actually funny when you think about it. Eight armed cops and my dad tries to outrun them through the kitchen. He got as far as the stove before a bald guy they called Pointy tackled him to the ground. I guess it wasn't funny at the time, what with my mom and my sister crying hysterically and my dad's face bleeding. But it's sure funny now, now that it's over and now that I hate him.

My mother says that Dad's a different kind of criminal. He's a white-collar criminal, which she says means he didn't really hurt anyone. (Anyone but me, I always say.) But they still threw him in jail. Our rip-off artist of a lawyer said he'd be in less trouble if he hadn't tried to run.

The thing is that Dad never really acted like a criminal. He laughed a lot, always kept his hair neatly combed, always wore a suit and tie, blah blah blah. And he had a smile that made you trust him, made you think everything would be all right. He even cried when they finally carted him off. That's something you never see in the movies—a bad guy who cries when the cops nab him. That was a rough thing to see. That was probably the hardest thing of all—watching Dad cry as cops threw him into the back of a squad car. Don't get me wrong. Right now, I hate the guy. But that was rough.

But enough about him. He blew it and now he has to live with it. So let me tell you what's really unfair: the fact that I, an entirely innocent human being, had to give up my easy life. I know, plenty of people live happy lives without being loaded. But if you go from the life of leisure that I once had, to the life of toil and drudgery that I have now, it's very, very hard.

My mom even forced me to get a job. She said I needed to start a college fund. Let me tell you what I really need: my old life back. That's it. I don't need college and I don't need a job. I need a house with a pool, and an expensive stereo, and a beach house. Just so I'm clear, let me say that I now have none of these things.